Unexpectingly Happily Ever After

Holly Kerr

Three Birds Press

Copyright © 2018 by Three Birds Press

All rights reserved.

No portion of this book may be reproduced in any form without written permission from the publisher or author, except as permitted by U.S. copyright law.

Unexpectingly Happily Ever After

Chapter One

> It's my belief that children should be seen rather than heard.
>
> *A Young Woman's Guide to Raising Obedient Children,*
> Dr. Francine Pascal Reid (1943)

"But Momma, we're going to be late. We *have* to go to soccer," Sophie whines. "Now. Right now."

"Yes, I know," I say, hanging tight to the patience needed to corral three 6-year-olds into the liquor store. "But Momma needs to pick something up so we need to pop in here a sec."

Sophie is right to be worried. Punctuality is not one of my virtues, but the LCBO is on the way to the soccer field, and it's not like they start to play right away. For an hour-long game, the kids maybe play for thirty-five minutes. There are warm-ups and pep talks and some parents insist on plugging their kids full of this super-protein smoothie before the game because they think these drinks are going to make their kid a better soccer player.

They don't work. I know, because one game I gave in to the pressure and mixed up a batch of this disgusting mess of ricotta, peanut butter, banana, beet, and chia seeds. And dark chocolate, which Lucy was very excited about.

As I sent the kids out onto the field, with full bellies and hyper from too much of the leftover chocolate, I felt like I deserved one of the hard-fought Good Parenting awards. But halfway through the game, Ben was pulled because of an upset tummy, and then Lucy woke me up in the night with a bad case of diarrhea, so we don't do smoothies anymore.

I do my best to ignore Sophie's litany of complaints as we maneuver the minefield that is the parking lot.

"Hey!" I shout, grabbing Sophie by the collar to pull her closer as a car swipes by a little too close for my liking. "Jeez! Kids here!"

"Is jeez like cheese?" Ben asks.

"No, jeez is for Jeezer Christ," Lucy corrects him.

I stare at my daughter who is full of self-importance. "Who is Jeezer Christ? Jee–I think all of you need to go to church!"

"Simon goes to church on the Holy High holidays," Sophie informs me.

"I think you're messing up your religions." Holding Ben by the hand and Sophie by the collar, Lucy is relegated to dangling from my arm. Literally dangling; all fifty-one pounds hanging off my arm.

At least it keeps her away from the cars.

Sometimes I wonder how I got to be here–as a mother of three active, energetic, amazing and extra-lovable kids; Sophie, Lucy, and Ben. They're mine. I did this.

I had help from J.B., but I did this. They came from *me*.

Sometimes the realization washes over me, usually at the worst possible moment, and I have to take a breath. *WTF.*

Being a mother had been my dream since I spent all my time playing with my Rub-a-Dub doll, but I never really considered what it meant to be a momma, especially to triplets. I love my babies more than life itself, but just being around them is exhausting. No one told me how tired I would be, or how, even six years after they were born, I still wouldn't be able to lose the last twelve pounds of baby weight, or even how my bladder seemed to have developed an incontinent stutter whenever I try to jump on the trampoline that
J.B. insisted we buy.

Actually, I think my sister might have told me about the bladder one, but I chose not to believe her.

"Lucy, wait! For once, can you at least try to walk at a normal pace?" I snap as Lucy breaks free and makes a run for the store, darting in front of a woman overloaded with grocery bags. "I've had a bitc–a long day, and I'm slow."

When I'm not corralling these three, I'm a kindergarten teacher. You'd think being responsible
for eighteen 5-year-olds would have given me the inside track to dealing with triplets, but no, not really. I found it's not something you can prepare for.

"But I'm fast because Momma needs her wine!" Lucy sings, pulling open the door and nearly taking out the woman with the bags.

"Sorry," I apologize to the woman. "Yes, Lucy, Momma always needs her wine."

Sophie takes my hand. "Is Momma tired?" she asks, surprisingly solicitous for a six-year-old.

"Yes, Momma is always tired, but it's okay because that's how Mommas are."

Lucy stops short at the swinging bar that blocks the entrance into the store, which also halts the woman with the bags.

"Move out of the way, Luce," I reach around and grab her shoulder so the woman can slide by her. I receive a scowl from both. "Now, push open the bar."

It's easy enough to push to get in, but it seems to be a mystery to a four-foot-tall kid.

"I want to push it!" Sophie demands, elbowing her sister aside.

"Wait your turn, Sophie," I tell her, attempting to use my best patient-mother voice, which is only
used in public. "Lucy first. Now you. And Benny. Hurry, someone else wants to come in."

One by one, my three children obediently push their way through the bar allowing them entrance to one of my favourite places. I smile apologetically at the older woman tapping her foot behind us as I follow them in.

Her tight-lipped smile tells me I'm not forgiven.

As the kids explode through the bar, the cashiers stare at us with a collection of expressions.

The *Aw, aren't they cute?* smile to the *Lady, control your kids* grimace.

I've seen them all before.

If my kids aren't already noticeable enough in their bright yellow soccer jerseys, which clash horribly with their curly, red hair, the commotion we cause is just another way of telling the world the Bergen triplets
have arrived.

I swear my heart stops beating every time I let the kids loose in a store. What will they break? What kind of chaos will they create? Will I lose them?

When they were younger, it had been the fear of the dreaded temper tantrum. Especially from Sophie. She's the most energetic and the most affectionate of the three, constantly showering me and her brother and sister with kisses, but she has a temper. Lucy and Ben are more level and calm, but Sophie is like a bouncy ball–up and down, up and down.

Doesn't make me love her any less.

I used to try and keep them with me, going so far to strap them into the stroller long after they had grown out of it. J.B. had found me the best stroller when I was pregnant, one that actually had four seats, so that I
had extra room to put the diaper bag or anything else.

Of course, Sophie couldn't be trusted to sit alone. I only made that mistake once, after she left a trail of Cheerios, Goldfish crackers, and the contents of my purse behind me through the mall.

"Okay, just over here, guys. *No running*! Sophie!"

"Momma, I *told* you that I'm not a *guy*," Lucy informed me. "I'm a *girl*."

"I'm well aware that you are in fact, a girl." I trot over to the sparkling wine section, with the three of them following close behind. A man stands idly before the shelves. "But I use *guys* as a gender-neutral term
of endearment, so I mean all three of you when I say it."

"I'm a girl too!" Sophie cries, skidding to a halt beside the man. "But Ben's not. He has a *penis!*"

The man reels back at the word, with an incredulous expression at me.

No sweet nicknames for body parts in our house. And unfortunately, Sophie has an odd love of the word
penis.

"Yes, he does," I agree grimly, with an apologetic glance at the man. "Help me look. I need a bottle of prosecco. It's black with a yellow label."

"What's prosciutto?" Ben asks. I continually wonder how my sweet son survived his time in my womb with his more rambunctious sisters. But Lucy and Sophie adore their brother, treating him with more respect and care than they do each other.

"Prosecco," I correct. "Prosciutto is that yummy cured ham that Uncle Cooper wraps around asparagus that you like."

"I don't like asparagus," Lucy announces. "It makes my pee smell funny."

"Yes, it does that." I glance around but the man has bolted. "Look, here it is. Come with Momma to pay, and let's go to soccer."

I can almost taste the dry, fruity taste of the prosecco sliding down my throat but I'll have to wait for it. The one time I brought wine to the soccer game, it was suggested by the coaches that I take my wine and drink it in the car.

It wasn't like I had been obvious. My sister Libby had bought me one of those handbags with the spout and the wine pocket, as a Christmas gift. I found it really worked with red Solo cups and a nice Gamay. And the
mothers I had shared the bottle with agreed it improved the game as well.

But tonight, the prosecco will have to wait. The plan is for me to take the kids to soccer, then race home where I have to snack, bath and bed them in record time, and then get myself over to Morgan's.

Even after all these years, Morgan, Brit, and I still manage to get together quite often, although not as frequently as before. Now it's more like every three weeks rather than weekly. Brit gets upset if we go longer than that.

Tonight we're foregoing our dinner out to meet for dessert at Morgan's house because her ten-month-old daughter has a cold and Morgan doesn't want to leave her. A bottle of prosecco will pair nicely with the lemon torte Morgan is providing.

Not making. Morgan, as awesome a friend as she is, is not a good cook.

I head to the cashier. "Are we ready?"

Sophie crouches and begins running in place. I groan, knowing what's coming and unable to stop it. "Soccer, soccer, soccer!" she chants, throwing up her hands and hitting Lucy on the chin. "Go, North York Blue!"

"Go, Team! Go!" Ben chimes in.

"Momma, Sophie hit me!" With eyes filled with tears, Lucy has a hand clamped to her chin.

I don't have to look around to know every person in the store is watching us. It's just how it is when I take the kids out.

"I know, sweetie. She didn't mean it." I draw Lucy in for a quick kiss. "She didn't mean it. She's just excited about your game. Which we have to get to."

"Aren't you excited?" Sophie bubbles.

"No. My chin hurts!" Lucy wails.

"I'm sorry." Instantly contrite, Sophie throws an arm around her sister. "Feel better?"

"Okay," Lucy says with a quick wipe of her eyes.

"She's okay, Momma," Ben assures me.

"I'm glad." A quick glance of my Fitbit tells me our extra time before the game has now run out. "Let's go. Go, team, go!"

"Go Blues!" Ben cheers and nudges Lucy.

"Go, team," she says weakly.

Note to self–going anywhere before a soccer game is a bad idea.

"Can I carry the bottle?" Sophie asks, for once asking politely rather than demanding. I hand the black bottle to her and grab another two for Lucy and Ben to carry. The Feria brand of sparkling wine is my favourite, so it's not like it will go to waste.

"Careful," I warn, but there's no need. Before owning *Thrice* with our friend Cooper, J.B. used to manage a bar, so the kids have grown up knowing bottles of alcohol are precious commodities.

Lucy leads the way to the cashier, holding her bottle proudly with two hands. It only takes a few minutes for the customer before us to finish his transaction, allowing the kids to carefully put the bottles on the counter.

"I can't sell you these," the cashier says, without a glance at the smiling faces of my children. He's older with a pinched face and a receding hairline that's borderline balding.

I'm trying to watch the kids at the same time as root through my oversized purse for my wallet, so it takes a moment for me to realize what he said. "I'm sorry?"

"I can't sell those bottles to you."

His face is creased into a frown, making him look extremely bad-tempered. But I smile anyway because working retail had taught me it's always easier to catch flies with honey than vinegar. "Can I ask why not?"

"Minors aren't allowed to touch the products," he barks.

"They're my kids."

"We were helping Momma carry her wine," Sophie says helpfully.

"Her prosciutto," Lucy adds.

"They're under the legal age, and it's illegal for them to touch the products," the man continues as if the kids hadn't spoken. "I can't sell you these bottles with them in the store."

My smile vanishes. "Are you fu–kidding me?"

"No."

"You want me to take them out of the store and come back to pay for these? They're six! What am I supposed to do with them? Put them on a leash in front of the store?"

"Not my problem. Next in line, please."

"Not your–Do you have kids?"

"None of your business."

"I bet you don't because you're so bad-tempered that no one would want to have sex with you."

His expression darkens even more.

"Please, leave the store, ma'am."

"Are you seriously kidding me? You're really refusing to sell me these because my kids carried them?" My voice rises dangerously, enough that the kids huddle together, watching me with wide eyes.

"I am. And if you don't leave the premises, I can have you charged."

I bark with laughter with that. "What's your name?"

"His tag says Bert, Momma," Sophie whispers.

"See how helpful my kids are?" I slap my hand on the counter. "I work hard for that and you just ruined it. Oh, I get it, 'it's all illegal,'" I mock, waving my hands. "But I promise you that your manager will hear about how much of an asshole you were to me. Come on, kids." I march away from the cashier, leaving the three bottles on the counter and a lineup of people behind me.

"You called him *asshole*, Momma," Ben whispers.

"Unfortunately, I did, Benny, because that's what he is. Let's get to soccer."

Chapter Two

Having a calm and serene mother makes it easy to raise a sweet, docile daughter.

A Young Woman's Guide to Raising Obedient Children
Dr. Francine Pascal Reid, (1943)

"It's bullshit. Utter bullshit. Can you believe that guy?" Even an hour later, I'm still shaking my head over the cashier. He refused to serve me–*me*, who used to work in a wine store and who the Ontario wineries owe a debt of gratitude for how much I drink.

I stand with two other mothers, as far away as we can be and still see the action, which involves one of two of the players running and kicking the ball, while the remainder of the teams chases behind them.

Nita shakes her head. I always hang out with Nita and Lisa at the soccer games. Our kids are about the same skill level–about mid-range.

I got tired of standing with the mothers of the kids who should be looking forward to tryouts for Toronto FC.

This is Toronto; there are some really good soccer players, even at this age.

"I've never even heard that rule," Nita says, clapping her hands as her son kicks the ball.

"It's a good rule," I concede. "But they're *six*. It's not like they were going to walk out with a bottle. Actually, I wouldn't put it past Sophie."

"They must have looked so cute, each with their own bottle," Lisa smiles. "Would they have made a fuss if you only had bought one bottle?"

"World War Three," I sigh. "It's not like it was going to go to waste. I'm meeting my girlfriends tonight, so that would have taken care of a bottle. Or maybe two."

"So J.B. is home tonight with the kids?" Nita asks, trying to act casual and failing miserably. "Is he coming to the game?"

My friend Nita, mother of Ben's best soccer friend, Tanner, has a thumping big crush on my husband.

J.B. says it's flattering. I'm fine with it. I kind of have to be since I have a teensy little crush on someone myself.

"Casey doesn't Dirk look amazing in those shorts," Lisa murmurs. Dirk is the twenty-five-year-old coach of the kids' team. A soccer player himself, Dirk has a great rapport with the kids and an even better one with the parents since all the mothers are too busy ogling his calves and thighs to bother complaining about the lack of playing their darlings receive.

Since I've become a mother, I can't help but notice some parents can be really annoying.

"Lovely," I murmur to Lisa before answering Nita. "And no, J.B. is at work, but he'll come home early. I've got a babysitter." I do a little dance to show my excitement.

"Lucky," Lisa sighs. "I can't seem to keep a babysitter. I find someone to watch Angelique for a night, but they're always too busy when I call again."

I don't respond. I like Lisa a lot, but I've had Angelique over for a play date and there would be no way I would ever agree to babysit her. There are still fingernail marks on the doorframe from where she tried to climb it.

"Doesn't J.B. ever get time off to come to the games?" Nita wonders.

How I deal with my husband's schedule is a mystery to most people. J.B. is the co-owner of *Thrice* restaurant, which means he works most nights. But since he owns it with our best friend Cooper, it makes it more manageable. Both of them work long hours, sometimes even twelve-hour days, but can always count on each other when they need time off.

J.B.'s time with the kids is in the mornings. He's in charge of dressing, feeding, and getting them to school, a bonus for me because I'm not much of a morning person. While he amuses the kids, I'm able to get ready for work.

"He'll come to the tournament," I say to Nita. I don't tell her that while J.B. loves to see the kids play, most of the other parents annoy the poop out of him.

"They're always trying to get reservations and free meals," J.B. had complained the last time he came to a game. "And their kids suck at soccer, so they should stop pretending they're going to be the next Lionel Messi."

"It's hard for him to get a whole night off," I continue. "Especially when Cooper—"

"Casey!" Lisa interrupts, pointing to the field. "Ben just fell."

"He didn't fall; that kid tackled him!" Nita exclaims, following me onto the field. Dirk is already running over to where Lucy is helping her brother to his feet.

"Where's Sophie?" I call with dismay. If Lucy is with Ben that means—

My second youngest triplet marches out from where she had been sitting on the sidelines, her curly, red pigtails bouncing with every step. The rest of the team follows her like she's the Pied Piper.

Her face is like a thundercloud.

"Sophie, don't!" I cry, but either she doesn't hear me or chooses to ignore me because she breaks into a run.

"Don't you ever hurt my brother!" she screams, making a beeline to the towheaded little brat who's laughing at the sight of poor Ben on the ground.

Sophie runs straight to the kid and drills a fist into his stomach.

"Oh no," I groan.

"Whose child is that?" The voice screeches across the soccer field, still dotted with the brightly coloured jerseys of the kids. "Whose daughter just did that to my son?"

The woman, all Lycra'ed out in a matching Lululemon running suit, strides onto the field and grabs Sophie's arm.

Grabs my daughter's arm.

I break into a run.

"Casey...don't," I hear Nita call after me.

"Get your hands off my daughter," I cry as I cross the field.

Ms. Lycra looks up with evil eyes. "Your daughter physically assaulted my son." She keeps a grip on Sophie, who looks ready to burst into tears at the manhandling. The "assaulted" boy rolls on the ground, holding his stomach.

With a visible smirk on his face.

"Your son physically attacked my son," I point out as Ben rushes to my side. "This is a non-contact sport if you hadn't noticed. Plus, they're six years old! Who teaches their kid to tackle at that age?"

The coach of the other team steps up to me, along with Dirk. "Just calm down now."

I glance at the coach, to the woman still holding my child. "He's your kid, isn't he? Tell your wife to get her hands off my daughter before I come over there and make her."

Lycra throws back her head in shock but releases Sophie who runs not to me, but to Ben. Lucy joins them.

"You should learn to control your children," the woman says, sounding as snotty as she looks. "Or don't have that many of them."

"You b–"

Dirk's hand on my shoulder is the only thing that stops me from demonstrating to both teams just how to make a proper tackle. "Casey," he warns. "Not a good idea in front of the kids."

I take a deep breath, then another. Conscious of the crowd thronged around me, I crouch in front of Ben. "Bennie, are you okay?"

His face is tear-stained, but he nods. I drop a kiss on his head and take his little hand in mine. "Sophie," I say in a firm voice. "Apologize to the boy for hitting him. You shouldn't have done that."

"But Momma, he hurt Ben..."

"He made him cry," Lucy chimes in.

My heart fills with pride at how they defend each other, but I don't let on yet.

"He did hurt your brother, and that's something he'll have to live with. I need you to apologize for hitting him, Sophie."

"That's all?" Lycra's expression is one of incredulousness. "That's how you're going to fix this?"

"It's a start, and it's better than what your hooligan of a son is doing," I snap back. I soften my voice. "Sophie."

"I'm sorry for hitting you," she says in a sullen voice.

I squeeze her hand and glance at Dirk, who looks unsure of what to do next.

"Such behaviour." A grandmotherly woman gasped. I'm not sure what team she's rooting for. "And from a little girl."

"That's what happens when you let girls play with the boys," reprimands her partner.

Most of the women in the crowd, me included, turn and glare at him.

"She should get suspended from the league," booms a voice from the opposite team.

"She's *six*," I hear Lisa from behind me.

"And the kid hurt her brother," Nita adds. "Game over if you ask me."

We look at Dirk. "That's probably a good idea," he says uneasily.

"Why?" Lycra sneers. "Your little girls afraid of what happens when they try and take out our best player?"

I can't believe this woman. "Yes," I say emphatically. "But I think you should worry what's going to happen if you or your kid ever lays a hand on one of my children again." I turn to Dirk. "I'm going to go now."

With that, I stalk to the car holding Sophie and Ben by the hands, with Lucy tucked up beside her sister.

"I would have hit the kid, but she got there first," Lucy said sullenly. I glance at her with surprise. I had no idea that she was so bloodthirsty. Sophie, yes, but Lucy is usually less aggressive than her sister.

"You can hit him next time," Sophie tells her sister proudly.

"He tackled *me*, so I should be the one to hit him." That is from Ben, never wanting to be left out of the sister bond.

"Nobody should hit anyone." I sigh.

"I didn't mean to cause a fuss," Ben says in a voice so low I have to bend to hear it.

"This is *not* your fault!"

"No, it's mine."

I flip to Sophie's sad face. "No, it's that snot-nosed little brat who thought he could take out one of my kids. Doesn't he know the wrath of the Bergen trips?"

"And their Momma," Lucy giggles. "You were really mad at that lady."

"Damn straight. Darn. I didn't mean damn. Darn straight." Try as hard as I might, I can't seem to stop the swearing in front of the kids.

"But why did you make me say sorry that I hit him?" Sophie wonders. "I'm not sorry."

We reach the car and I wait until all three are inside, tumbling into car seats, scrambling for seatbelts. I wait until they face me, two sets of identical brown eyes and one with blue and hazel. All three are wearing different expressions–sad, curious and faintly resentful. They're not identical but the similar features make no question that they belong together. All of them have part of me, whether it's Sophie's chin, Lucy's freckles along her cheeks along with my mixed eye colour, or the downturn of Ben's mouth.

They have part of J.B. as well, but I like to focus on the parts of *me*. After all, I'm the one who carried all three of them at once, making me as big and cumbersome as a manatee out of the water.

Then I take yet another deep breath, knowing I'm probably breaking most of the good parenting rules. "I'm not sorry you hit him either.

But don't tell anyone that. I love how the three of you defend each other and hope you never stop."

"So it's okay that I hit him?" Sophie asks with a confused tilt to her red head.

"No. It's never okay to hit someone." At least I got that part of the parent code right. "But if you do, make sure you don't get caught."

Chapter Three

> The day should end at a time for the mother to relax and reflect on the challenges of the day. Perhaps a hot bath. The use of alcohol is not considered an effective method of relaxation.
>
> *A Young Woman's Guide to Raising Obedient Children*
> Dr. Francine Pascal Reid, (1943)

"And then the mother kept screaming at *me* and refused to listen when I tried to point out how it was her son who started everything by knocking over Ben. We were winning the game, by the way," I finish my tale, sniffing appreciatively at the cabernet sauvignon Morgan had poured for me when I walked in. Another few mouthfuls and I'll need a refill.

I tuck my legs underneath me on the couch. We've taken over Morgan's living room with plates of lemon tart and brownies that J.B.

sent with me, as well as bottles of wine. Morgan's condo used to be a showplace of art and décor, tidy enough to be fastidious. I used to be afraid to walk barefoot around the place without a fresh manicure.

A lot has changed since Carson came along. Board books and squishy blocks have taken the place of Morgan's collection of Swarovski crystal butterfly figurines and Tiffany candlesticks, which have been relegated to gathering dust on the top shelf. There's a dollhouse set up in the corner of the room and a veritable world of Little People sets beside it.

I shudder when I see a doll's head tucked among the glass balls Morgan has arranged in a bowl on the table behind the couch and make a mental note to remove it for her later.

"Why do parents always use *we* when they talk about their kids' sports?" Brit asks, crossing her long legs on the couch beside me. "*You* don't play soccer, so why do you say *we* won?"

I stare at Brit over the rim of my glass, swallowing the last few mouthfuls before holding my glass out for Morgan to refill.

Brit Spears–she dropped the 'ney in the 90s when the other Britney Spears became famous–and I have been friends since ninth-grade gym class where we discovered that it was easy to get out of playing basketball with a well-timed groan about our "monthly friend" while holding our stomach.

I've never been one for sports.

The two of us are now well into our twenty-seventh year of friendship, enduring her parents' divorce, my mother, her stepmother, Brit's three weddings and subsequent divorces, and my pregnancy and resulting three children. I still love her, but she can be a bitch sometimes.

The cry of the baby sends Morgan running out of the room.

"No more talk about kids tonight," Brit says, waving a forkful of tart through the air. A pastry flake drops onto her blouse. "That's all you seem to talk about these days. You need a life, Casey!"

I've lost track of how often Brit has told me that.

"I have a life, Brit. And my kids are a big part of it, which you'd understand if you had kids." And pretended to be a better friend, I add silently.

"Do you blame me? After watching what you went through during your pregnancy? And you?" Brit turns to Morgan, who has returned with Carson.

"What did I do?" Morgan asked as she settles onto the couch. Without even asking, she hands me Carson.

"Hello, pretty baby," I coo, full of smiles. Carson reaches out and grabs a fistful of my red hair. Morgan hands me a warm bottle and as I offer it to the baby, her blue eyes blink sleepily at me. I tuck her closer and Morgan covers her with a blanket.

There's nothing better than holding a warm little body in your arms.

"This." Brit waves her arms. The baby has distracted me and I have no idea what Brit is upset about. "The two of you are baby crazy. Still!"

Ah, yes. Her usual rant.

"For you, Morgan, to willingly go through all this without a husband..." Brit shakes her blond hair, still so full and lush from her blowout two days ago. "I really don't understand."

"How do you get your hair to stay so nice?" I ask as I idly stroke Carson's foot. Baby feet are the cutest things ever. Her toes are tucked into the yellow onesie I gave her, passed down from Lucy. "There's no way my hair would stay that way after a day, let alone two."

"You have difficult hair," Brit says with a smug smile.

I meet Morgan's gaze and hide my smile. Attack averted. Every time we get together these days, Brit doesn't hesitate in expressing her displeasure at the fact Morgan and I have kids. I think she's jealous, and I've called her out on it more than once, but it didn't go anywhere because Brit didn't want to discuss it.

I'm used to her comments about the kids, seeing as how I've had almost seven years to get used to it. But Carson isn't even a year old yet. My kids were three when Brit eventually stopped moaning and groaning about all the *changes,* but Carson seemed to have instigated the resurgence.

Especially since Morgan had Carson on her own.

Not that Morgan's the first woman to have a baby out of wedlock, but I like to think I gave her the idea.

When I was thirty-five, I underwent a bit of a crisis, thinking that my biological clock was about to run out of batteries. This was thanks to a long out-of-print book my mother gave to me, called *A Young Woman's Guide to the Joy of Impending Motherhood.* It came out in the 1940s.

A lot has changed since then, including the age women have babies.

After I read the book cover to cover, I freaked out and decided I needed to get pregnant *immediately.* Of course, it's never that easy, especially when you discover your current boyfriend "cuddled" up with another woman at a wedding.

They weren't exactly cuddling but I've changed the story to make it more PG since I'm the mother of young children now.

At the time, I was used to dating disasters and quickly bounced back. I was quick to come up with a few plans to make a baby happen; sperm donors, artificial insemination, and random guys on the subway. The best idea was having a baby with my ex-boyfriend, David, who by that time had realized he was gay.

That would have worked, had it not been for a drunken night with J.B.

I realize the doctor who wrote the book was a quack, but I still blame her for the stress I went through. I don't credit her for me getting pregnant because that would have happened anyway.

Or maybe not, if I'd had a better history of dating. I like to think J.B. and I would have eventually gotten together, but who knows? It took long enough.

Morgan fell in love with my kids at the same time she fell out of love with her boyfriend at the time, Derek. But she stuck with him for two more years because she wanted that unconditional love that I had from the kids, and he seemed to be her best bet.

Knowing you're the most important person in your child's life is scary as hell sometimes, but really amazing all of the time.

Morgan and Derek finally broke up, and unbeknownst to me and Brit, Morgan began researching IVF. I finally caught wind to what she was doing about six months later. My suggestion was for her to contact my former boyfriend, David, who now lives with his boyfriend Marco in San Francisco. At one time David suggested *he* father my unborn children, but that's part of the long story.

It took Morgan a couple years and many rounds of IVF to get pregnant. She's thanked me countless times for supporting her through the ordeal.

Brit on the other hand...

To give Brit credit, she kept her mouth relatively shut until about six months after Carson was born. And then she resumed the complaining about how we're too occupied with the kids, have no time for her, need to start focusing on ourselves, etc, etc.

In Brit's defense, she's gone through three weddings and three divorces since I got pregnant. I know part of her complaints stem from the fact that she's jealous and lonely, and having a really rough time in the relationship department. At least that's what I keep telling myself.

I also keep reminding myself that while Brit is self-absorbed and a bitch, she's also my oldest friend, and I do love her.

"So," Brit begins, setting her plate on the table beside her. "You know I'm getting married again."

"I seem to recall hearing something about that." Morgan leans over to check if Carson has fallen asleep, but I catch sight of her smirk. The only thing Brit loves more than attention is planning her wedding. I think three weddings and an engagement is proof that she likes the weddings more than the actual marriages.

"Yes, well, I've decided what I want to do for my stagette."

I don't bother hiding my groan. "Really, Brit? It's the fourth time. I'm too tired to plan on anything more than a night out at Boston Pizza."

"Please tell me you don't go there," Brit sniffs. "You say you love your kids but you take them there?"

"What's wrong with Boston Pizza? The fish tacos are really good, and they have these cactus chips that I love."

"I like the pizza," Morgan chimes in. "It's not as good as Cooper's but nothing really is."

I wonder how many arguments Morgan has prevented between Brit and me over the years. I might have known Brit longer, but Morgan was my university roommate, which is a different friendship than a high school best friend. Morgan is solid, a good fit for my less than practical side.

I've been called flaky, flighty, and a dreamer. Having a practical friend is always good.

I shift the sleeping baby in my arms. "You should try this new pasta Cooper's put on the menu. It's to die for!"

"I eat too much pasta, but I can't seem to stop myself. I'm sure Carson is going to have a wheat intolerance from how much I ate when I was pregnant."

"I don't think it works that way because–"

"We're talking about *me*!"

Carson's eyes flutter open at the sound of Brit's shriek, and her grip tightens on my hair.

"Shh," Morgan and I admonish in unison.

"Sorry," Brit says, dropping her voice. "But I need to tell you what's going on so we can book it."

"You honestly want a fourth bachelorette party? We can just go out for a nice dinner and have a quiet night. Do you really think this is...?" I don't continue because Brit is looking at me like I've sprouted another head. I'm not sure what I want to say anyway. Is it socially acceptable to have a fourth stagette?

Brit wouldn't give a good goddamn even if that was the case.

"What do you want to do?" I ask with resignation.

"I want to go to Las Vegas," Brit announces. "And both of you are coming with me."

CHAPTER FOUR

Children's diets should remain consistent with no new foods introduced until their palates are established, which is around the onset of puberty.

A Young Woman's Guide to Raising Obedient Children
Dr. Francine Pascal Reid, (1943)

"So Brit thinks I can drop everything and go to Vegas with her."

It's the next night, and I'm perched on a stool in the kitchen watching J.B. prepare dinner. I'm still shaking my head at Brit's plan for the three of us to spend a weekend in Las Vegas together.

It's totally unrealistic, and the logistics of figuring out how to make it happen is already giving me a headache. But somewhere, deep inside me, the twenty-five-year-old party Casey thinks a trip like that would be amazing. To get on a plane and take off for a few days...

Impossible. I'm a mother now. Selfless, responsible...

"Sounds like a good idea," J.B. says.

The twenty-five-year-old party boy is obviously still wide awake inside him.

"What are you talking about? I've got the kids to worry about, not to mention my job, which wouldn't really matter because she's talking about going for a weekend, but there's the restaurant and the kids and you..." I list, finishing one hand and starting on the other.

J.B. has a rare Friday night off. He had suggested the two of us going out, but I told him I'd rather stay at home with the kids because I know he likes spending as much time with them as he can.

Plus, if we stay home, that means J.B. will cook.

"It's her *fourth* wedding and I'm sure there'll be more to come. How can she want to go have a big hoopla for something's that not even going to last?"

Even though the hoopla would be fun while it lasted.

"How do you know it's not going to last?" J.B. admonishes. "Who's she marrying this time?"

"Justin somebody. Don't you love it? Britney and Justin?" I shake my head at J.B.'s blank expression. "Britney Spears and Justin Timberlake? The cutest couple of the 90s? Or maybe it was the 2000s. No? You're such a boy."

"You like me being a boy." He wiggles his eyebrows, making me smile.

"Sometimes. Did I tell you that Sophie told the whole LCBO that Ben has a penis? Why don't you get outbursts like that?"

"I get outbursts."

"Do they involve penises and vaginas?"

"Not really, no."

"I'm going to tell them to come to talk to you when they want to know about sex," I promise.

"Then our children will never have sex because I'll put the fear of God into them."

I sit on the stool at the counter as J.B. pours himself a glass of Cabernet Sauvignon and begins to prepare dinner. I love watching him in the kitchen. The graceful way he moves between counter and stove, the way he cleans up as he goes. Watching his knife fly through the mountain of vegetables, most of which the kids won't eat.

None of them like the same thing. Carrots and corn and brussels sprouts for Sophie; peppers and tomatoes and celery for Ben; onions and cauliflower for Lucy.

The variety makes for a crowded vegetable drawer in the fridge.

"Do you want wine or should I make you a martini?" J.B. asks.

"It's Friday night," I say, leaving out the *duh*.

He reaches up to the cupboard where we keep the liquor. It's a good-sized cupboard, considering he used to be a bartender and likes to hone his craft and I like to drink. I quite like being the recipient of his creations.

"Who helped last time?" he mutters to himself as he pulls the gin out of the freezer.

"Ben," I tell him, thinking back to last Sunday when J.B. gave a Ben a lesson on how to make a whiskey sour.

Yes, our six-year-old children are budding bartenders. They like to help in the kitchen as well, but all three are fascinated by the science of mixology. At least that's how J.B. justifies it.

"It's science," he said last weekend as Ben measured Canadian Club into a shot glass. "It's not like he's going to taste it.

I didn't tell him that I had seen Sophie stick her finger in my drink more than once.

After determining that it's Sophie's turn to learn how to make a drink, he calls to her to help him.

"We're not the best parents, are we?" I ask. "Promoting alcohol?"

"It's a teachable skill," J.B. argues with a grin. "Plus, they're being helpful and considerate, because they know Momma needs a drink after a long week."

"It's a life lesson," I add. "It's good to know that the three of them will be able to support themselves on a bartender's salary if we can't afford to keep them."

"Why can't you keep us?" Sophie wonders as her red head pops up on the other side of the counter. "Because if you can't, I want to live with Cooper. Lucy and Ben will want to live with Aunt Libby, but I want Cooper."

Along with owning *Thrice* with J.B., Cooper and his wife Emma used to be our roommates. Or rather, Cooper and J.B. used to be roommates, and I rented out the basement apartment in Cooper's house. And then Emma moved in. And then J.B. and I had the trips, and it became a very crowded household.

When the kids were about a year and a half, J.B. and I got our own place. Doing the mortgage thing really makes me feel like a grown-up, something J.B. always shakes his head about. "Shouldn't having three babies make you feel like a grown-up?"

Having three babies makes me feel awesome. And exhausted.

It's been years, but there are times I miss Coop and Emma being around. We see them all the time, but I really miss Cooper making me breakfast on the weekend. I've more than repaid him for the free food he provided for me; when the triplets were two, I agreed to become a surrogate for Emma and Cooper. Atticus and Aiden are now four, energetic and excitable, sweetly adorable with their shock of blond hair and identical features and look more like Emma than Cooper.

The kids adore each other. We've always been open with the situation–the boys came from my tummy, but belong to Cooper and

Emma–and the kids accept the explanation, even though none of them really understand it.

"I'm sure Cooper'll be happy to hear that you want to live with him if we get rid of you," I say to Sophie. "Maybe a little frightened at the quickness of your decision but pleased you picked him."

"Don't worry, you're not going anywhere," J.B. assured her, setting the jar of olives on the counter.

"Ooh, I love olives." Sophie beams, rubbing her hands together.

"Since when does she like olives?" J.B. turns to me.

I can't comment on how a father should know what their children like to eat, because I had no idea Sophie even knew what an olive was.

Actually, she'd helped make martinis before and I like my olives. But I had no idea she knew they were a food to be eaten outside an alcoholic beverage.

"Maybe she had them on the pizza last week?" I guess.

J.B. speared an olive and offered the green globe to Sophie, who plucked it from the fork with relish. "Mmm. More, please."

"Help me make Momma's drink first. What's in a martini?"

I should be afraid if this is what J.B. considers a teachable moment, but I only look at him with love.

He didn't have to be here. He hadn't wanted to be a father. Neither one of us planned on a drunken evening between friends resulting in anything more than a fond memory.

When I found out I was pregnant, J.B. hadn't handled things well, and he'd be the first to admit it. Then, of course, I got mad. And stubborn. The first time he asked me to marry him, I said no.

It hadn't been much of a proposal. More of a *this is what we're going to do* type of conversation, which never goes well for me. I don't like being told what to do. I even informed J.B. that I expected absolutely nothing from him. I was fully prepared and committed to raising the baby on my own.

Of course, that was back when I had no idea I was carrying triplets.

I'll always be grateful that J.B. came around. And that I accepted his second proposal. Despite the rocky beginning, J.B. and I have made it work. We have three beautiful children and a happy, albeit a little unconventional marriage.

"James Bond drinks vodka martinis but Momma likes gin," Sophie answers J.B.'s question.

"That's right," J.B. says, sounding more like a teacher than I do. "And James Bond likes his martini shaken, but we like to stir Momma's because it bruises the gin if you shake it."

"Like Ben's bruise from that kid tripping him in soccer," Sophie says.

"Kind of." J.B. glances at me. He had been furious Ben had been hurt during the soccer game by some snot-nosed kid with a mom whose Botox injections impeded her ability to parent–his words, not mine. But he was pleased as punch that Sophie defended her brother and thinks we should encourage such behaviour.

The teacher in me frowns on encouraging it, and we tabled the discussion without coming to a resolution. Hopefully, it won't be an issue again.

He places a shot glass in front of the little bruiser, with her adorable red curls and mischievous eyes. Both Sophie and Ben have inherited J.B.'s brown eyes, with Lucy sharing my trait of one blue, one hazel eye. "Two ounces of gin, please," J.B. instructs.

"Is that how much James Bond drinks?" Sophie wants to know.

"And why do you teach them about James Bond?" I wonder aloud. "He's not the most kid-friendly character."

UNEXPECTINGLY HAPPILY EVER AFTER

Sophie runs her hand along an imaginary table. "He's smooth, Momma. As cool as the other side of the pillow."

"Is that what you teach them?" I ask faintly.

"A knowledge of James Bond will only help the kids in any trivia game," J.B. reassures me as he dribbles vermouth into the glass. "Now we plop the olives in the glass." J.B. holds the jar out for Sophie.

I laugh as both Sophie and J.B. make plopping sound effects as the olives sink into the gin.

"And now we add a couple of spoonfuls of the juice from the olives because Momma likes it dirty."

J.B. glances at me over Sophie's head and wiggles his eyebrows. I smile primly in return.

"And now we stir." J.B. hands Sophie a plastic stir stick and she attacks her task with gusto. Gin spills over the side of the glass. "That's good," he says hastily, waving her away before I lose more of the drink before I get to drink it.

"Let's give her more olives," Sophie suggests.

"And another for you?"

"Okay! One for Momma," Sophie adds another to my glass, and the alcohol wavers just under the brim. "And one for me." She pops it into her mouth.

"Thanks for helping, Super Soph," J.B. says, dropping a kiss on the top of her head.

"Anytime, Daddy." She throws her arms around his waist and gives him a squeeze before running out of the room.

The love on his face warms my heart.

He takes a sip before passing me the glass. "She makes a good martini."

"She's learned from the best."

"Either they're going to have a drinking problem or they're never going to touch the stuff," he says.

"Hopefully a happy medium between the two."

Once I'm content with my drink, J.B. turns back to his dinner preparations, scooping up the julienned vegetables and throwing them in the pan. The smell of garlic reminds me of a time, long ago, when I sat and watched J.B. cook for me. He made a spicy pork stir-fry for me that night. Tonight its chicken.

It seems like yesterday but feels like a lifetime ago.

We made a family. A pretty good one.

"Why can't you go to Vegas?" J.B. asks out of nowhere.

He asks that just as I'm taking a sip of my martini. I'm so surprised that I choke, spraying gin over my hand holding the glass. Such a waste.

"You're telling me to get on a plane and fly to Vegas just because Brit tells me to? I have work, kids, soccer games; you have work, kids...There's no way I can do it."

I keep my voice incredulous, rather than let the regret seep in.

I'm not sure why I would feel regret. This will be Brit's fourth wedding, which means she's already had three bachelorette/stagette/adult showers involving copious amounts of alcohol and organized by yours truly.

Or at least, I followed the detailed instructions Brit gave me.

Maybe I hadn't been that into celebrating during the first time around, but in my defense, I was newly pregnant and suffering from morning/noon/night sickness which resulted in me being hospitalized for dehydration. Not a fun time. Add in the cold war that had been going on with J.B. at the time and it wasn't the best time of my life. But I more than made up for it for Brit's second stagette. I still have bad memories of the hangover.

Giving the vegetables a stir, J.B. steps from behind the counter to the doorway. "Five minutes until dinner," he bellows.

"What's five minutes?" Sophie calls back.

"When the big hand is on the one, and the little hand is on the six," he replies. "Six oh five."

"Okay, Daddy!" Ben chimes back over the sounds of *Paw Patrol*.

For some reason I find the sight of my husband parenting our children, even small things like calling them for dinner, an incredible turn on. He's still so good-looking. But then again, his body didn't take a beating from birthing three children all at once.

"What makes you think you can't go to Vegas?" J.B. asks again, back to stir the veggies. He slides the sliced chicken into the pan and is rewarded by the sizzling sounds of frying meat. "I'll talk to Coop, see if I can take a couple of nights off. I think it'll do you good."

I stare at my husband over the rim of my glass. It's not that J.B. isn't supportive or considerate–he actually understands the equality of the partnership of marriage better than I ever thought he would. Other than a hate of doing laundry, things are pretty equal when it comes to chores in our little household. But it's one thing to fold a basket of clothes or clean a bathroom. It's another to keep track of three 6-year-olds, responsible for their care and feeding for hours at a time. J.B. is perfectly capable of doing it but never has.

Doesn't he know how exhausting the kids can be? Regardless of how much I love them and how fun they are at times, they make me tired.

Very tired.

I drain the martini, plucking an olive out of the bottom. "Are you serious?"

"Why wouldn't I be serious? You worried I can't handle it?"

I only laugh, refraining from saying anything because Lucy flies into the kitchen. Literally flies, since she's wearing her prized Wonder Woman cape that my sister got her for her birthday.

"Yum, olives," she cries. Before I can stop her, she reaches into to my glass and snags one of the last remaining olives.

Olives that have been immersed in two ounces of high-quality Henricks gin.

"Lucy, no!" I cry grabbing for her hand, but not before she pops the olive into her mouth.

She frowns as she chews. "It tastes funny."

I look at J.B. with horror. But J.B. only laughs. "Well, she won't do that again."

"You think I'm going to leave you with them for a weekend?" I demand.

"I'm not the one who left a boozy olive there for her, like some squishy Skittle."

"It's nothing like a Skittle!"

"The kid loves olives. Don't you, Lucy Goosey."

Lucy grins as her father ruffles the red curls. "I love olives!"

"Can I have an olive?" Ben asks, popping up under my arm and reaching for my glass. "I like them."

"You better give him one too," J.B. sighs.

"I'm not giving him my olives."

"Just one, Momma. Like Lucy."

"These aren't regular olives," I say, not wanting to explain what makes them so different.

"They're Momma olives," Lucy says proudly. "They're *yummy*."

"I want one," Sophie sings.

I have no idea where she came from. Now all three of them are grouped around me, with expectant expressions on their face. J.B. shrugs.

"It won't hurt them."

I exhale audibly. Before I can change my mind, I pluck the last two remaining olives out of my martini glass and hand them to my daughter and son.

"Yum!" they cry in unison, popping the green fruit into their mouths.

"Do you ever think we're not the best parents?" I ask J.B., slipping off the stool with glass in hand in case the kids want to lick the dregs of gin or something.

J.B. laughs. "We should write a *What Not to Do* for parents. It'd be a bestseller."

"We'd get charged for something," I say gloomily.

Chapter Five

> Subsequent children should be planned at regular intervals.
>
> *A Young Woman's Guide to Raising Obedient Children*
> Dr. Francine Pascal Reid, (1943)

Later, after dinner and a movie and bath and bedtime, after I've fallen asleep twice trying to get through an episode of *Scandal*, J.B. curls up around me in bed.

"You're a good momma, you know." His hand slips under my old university T-shirt.

"You're just saying that because you're looking to get some action."

"I'm saying it because it's true," he argues. "I'm grabbing your beautiful boob because I'd like some action."

"Oh, I suppose." I give a mock sigh and roll over onto my back.

We've been married just over six years and I love that he still wants me. Of course, his schedule and the obstacles of having three little people capable of wandering into our room makes sexy time a bit of a challenge, but J.B. has shown his creativity more than once.

He leans over to kiss me, and I run my hand through his dark hair. The waves are mostly gone now, cut into a brutally short "grown-up" hairstyle. I miss his long hair.

I don't miss the man-bun, even though I have to admit he kind of rocked it.

J.B. continues his exploration, and I'm thinking it's time to get rid of my sleep shirt when he suddenly stops kissing me.

"You ever think about having another one?"

"Another breast?"

"Another *baby*."

I slide out from under him quicker than I did the time Lucy wandered into our bedroom while she was sleepwalking.

"What? *Why?* Why?" I demand from the far side of the bed. "And don't even say the word–the last time I just *wished* for a baby and look what happened!"

"The kids are older now...They're always talking about having a younger brother or sister." J.B. reaches for me but I keep moving until I'm standing beside the bed, as far away from him without leaving the room.

"They don't talk to *me* about that! And they should because it's *my* decision." I fold my arms across my chest, effectively telling J.B. sexytime is over without saying a word.

"It was your decision before," he says mildly, sitting up. "I think I should have a say in it this time."

"There's no *this time*! Or that time. There was one time," I hold up a finger. "One time getting pregnant. That's it."

"You're forgetting the surrogacy," J.B. points out.

"One time with you!"

"So you haven't thought about it?"

I push away the feeling of holding Carson in my arms. "*No!* Why the holy heck would I? Do I have a death wish?"

"Do you want to maybe think about it?"

My *no* is about to snap off the tip of my tongue when I catch sight of the hopeful expression on his face. "What's going on? Where's this coming from?"

"That's not a no," he says with a smile, ignoring my question. He reaches a tentative hand out to me.

"That's a *you should stay away from my boobs tonight.*" I tighten my arms across my chest.

"Oh. Really?" His hand hangs limply in the air until he pulls it back.

"Boobs or baby, big guy."

J.B. gives a nervous laugh. "Kind of can't have one without the other."

"Oh, *funny.*"

"C'mon, Casey."

It takes a few more minutes of wistful cajoling before I finally allow myself to be pulled back into bed. "I guess it was bad timing for this conversation," J.B. says ruefully.

"You *think?*"

"Kind of like that morning way back when, after we had the sex, and then you started spouting off to Cooper and Emma about how you wanted to have a baby?"

I laugh. For years, I'd been consumed with the desire to have a baby to the dismay of my friends. They had no issues about me becoming a mother, but their concerns were how I had planned to go about it. No waiting for happily ever after for me. No, I had been impatient enough to have gone through ill-thought-out plans to conceive which involved a random dude I met on the subway, the best ex-boyfriend ever, and a turkey baster as a last resort.

It had been ironic that I'd never given that night with J.B. a second thought until the three positive pregnancy tests had stared me in the face.

Ironic, or a good example of how obsessed I'd been about becoming a mother.

"You were so freaked out," I reminisce. "I bet you still think I poked a hole in that condom."

"You can't prove that you didn't."

I laugh again, forgetting my ire and snuggling against him. "Using an expired condom was the best thing I ever did."

"I agree." He kisses me and I let him, even relaxing enough to allow his hand to begin to wander again.

"So have you thought about it?" he whispers into my neck.

"You need to stop talking."

"Momma?"

"I said you need to stop talking," I hiss.

J.B.'s hand stops. "That wasn't me."

Both of us look to the end of the bed where a small figure in Wonder Woman pajamas is rubbing her eyes. "What's wrong, Lucy?"

"I can't sleep."

"Seemed to be doing okay when I checked on you earlier," J.B. says under his breath as he eases away from me.

I sigh. "C'mon up."

J.B. pulls the blankets away and Lucy hops onto the bed with a grin on her face. At least once a week, one of the kids will end up in bed with us.

It makes sexy time even more difficult.

"We should get a lock on the door," J.B. mutters as Lucy cuddles between us.

"They picked the bathroom lock once when I was in there," I remind him. "There's no keeping them out."

"I lost Lucy," a new voice whispers from the doorway.

"She's here, Benny. C'mon in." Ben runs to J.B.'s side of the bed with a big smile as his father picks him up and swings him across. Soon Ben and Lucy are snuggled together in the middle of the bed, providing an insurmountable obstacle for J.B.'s wandering hands.

"Love you," I say softly, smiling across the curly heads at J.B.

"Love you too, Momma," Ben replies.

J.B. rolls his eyes and sits up, swinging his legs out of the bed.

"Where are you going?"

"Water. And to make sure Sophie's tied down. There's not room enough for three of them in here."

I watch as he pads to the door, hear his footsteps descend the stairs.

Was he really serious about another baby?

I can tell from Lucy's breathing she's already asleep and Ben is close behind. I should carry them back to their beds, but it feels nice to have them here with me.

For the few weeks after they were born when I was trying to nurse them, J.B. would often bring them to bed with us, and we would play pass the baby. Their feeding schedules had been horrible–none of them ever wanted to eat together, so it was as if I always had a baby on my breast. That was until a tearful thirty-two hours with no sleep, after which I sent J.B. on a mission to find a twenty-four-hour WalMart and not come home without baby formula.

I like the smell of the kids in bed with me. Clean and fresh, smelling faintly of the apple honey baby soap I still use on them.

Do I want another baby? Does J.B.?

I lay in bed, listening to Ben's even breathing and Lucy's soft snores until I pull myself out of the warmth of the blankets to find J.B.

"Were you serious?" I demand, following the sound of the tap to the kitchen.

J.B. jumps at the sound of my voice. "That I needed I drink? Yeah."

"About a baby."

"You told me to stop talking about that."

"I just want to know why? Why now?"

J.B. leans against the counter as he drinks from the glass of water. "I don't know," he says finally, staring at the half-empty glass like it has the answers for him. "I've been thinking how cute they were, how much fun—"

"Fun?" I interrupt incredulously.

"It was fun, wasn't it? Some of the times. When we had enough sleep. Trying to figure things out, just you and me..."

"We can try to figure out other things," I suggest. "Like an IKEA bookcase."

"So you don't want another one?"

I heave a sigh. "Honestly? I haven't given it a thought. I wanted a baby for so long and then we had three and I love them so much and I never thought about more."

"But you thought about getting pregnant again? For Cooper and Emma."

"But I didn't have to keep those babies."

I admit, I do—did—enjoy being pregnant despite the side effects, but it had been tough dealing with my own kids while carrying two of Emma and Cooper's. At this moment, I can't imagine how difficult it would be to be pregnant while running around after the three of them.

"I guess I just thought I was done," I finish.

"You don't have to be. You're still young. We both are."

"I don't feel it. I'm almost forty-two." I rub my ear, feeling the hoop earring that I forgot to take out. I forget a lot of things—my phone, my lunch, and sometimes even going to the bathroom will get pushed out of my mind if I'm distracted by the kids.

Those three mean the world to me. Why wouldn't I want another?

"Could we afford it?" I wonder, sounding practical for the first time in my life. "Not that I'm saying anything, but four would be expensive. And, oh my god, what if I had more than one!"

I almost miss the look of horror that flits across J.B.'s face.

"The restaurant is doing great," J.B. reminds me, smoothing out his expression. "We're thinking about opening another one. Look, Case, we don't have to talk about this right now. It's the middle of the night."

"It's actually only eleven thirty," I tell him. "And it's really the last thing I want to talk about."

"I can take a hint," he says stiffly.

"We could talk about other things," I suggest, moving close enough to hook my fingers in the waistband of his boxers. "It's still early for you."

He glances at me with narrowed eyes. "It's not for you."

"I'm still awake. Or maybe we could not talk at all." In case he didn't know where I was going with this, I slide my hand down the front of his boxers. "Are you awake enough? Seems like you're a little sleepy, but I could wake you up all the way."

"Are you kidding me? A couple of minutes ago you jumped out of the bed for mentioning babies." J.B. says incredulously. But he doesn't push me away. "Now you're trying to tell me the topic turns you on?"

"Those two kids pushed you out of the bed, not me. And I'm tired of talking. Wouldn't it be more fun to practice, without really practicing? Especially without an audience?"

My husband is a smart man and knows a good thing when he gets it. Without another word, J.B. grabs my other hand and pulls me against him.

Chapter Six

> Mothers should refrain from allowing children to join them in mundane errands as it fosters a sense of complacency among children.
>
> *A Young Woman's Guide to Raising Obedient Children*
> Dr. Francine Pascal Reid, (1943)

The next morning, J.B. whisks Ben and Lucy out of the bed before the two of them decide it would be a fun thing to do to wake up Momma. When I finally crawl out of bed, still with a smile on my face from the kitchen-apades that went on last night, I jump into high gear right away.

J.B. is heading to the restaurant later this afternoon, but we have much to do before then. Brunch with Emma, Cooper and the boys. Grocery shopping. A possible play in the park.

My mind heads back to what J.B. asked me last night.

He wants to have another *baby*?

What is he thinking? How can he think I have enough energy to deal with another one? And what if it's more than one?

That thought is scarier than any Stephen King novel.

What would life be like with *five* kids? I've been pregnant twice in my life and both times I ended up with multiples. I skirt over the fact that with the surrogacy, it was Cooper and Emma's fault. They put two egg/sperm combos inside me, and that's what came out. My uterus is obviously a playground for babies. The more, the merrier.

So chances are if I got pregnant again, I'd be having more than one. And that is unimaginable.

There's not enough time in the day to deal with the crying and feeding and putting them into bed…or giving them baths. How am I supposed to bathe *five* kids? They'd be the most disgustingly dirty children because I wouldn't be able to clean them on a regular base.

"Are you okay, Case?" J.B. asks as we drive to Emma and Cooper's. He catches me staring unseeingly out the window as I picture five little Pig-Pens running through the house, each with their own cloud of dirt.

"Fine."

"You don't seem fine."

I glance incredulously at J.B. How can he be so casual about this? He asked me to disrupt my life, turn my body inside out *again*. "Were you serious last night?"

He frowns. "What about? Oh. That."

I glance behind me. It's quiet, and while that's usually a bad thing, in this case, Lucy and Ben are watching something on Ben's mini iPad, while Sophie has headphones attached to her iPod.

The teacher in me hate that children of this generation seem to have developed an addiction to screens, but the mother in me is often grateful for the quiet it provides.

"So you want another baby."

J.B. shrugs. "I thought we could think about it."

"But *why*?"

"Because I love our kids?"

"Do you love them enough to have three more?"

"Seriously, what are the chances of that?" he asks with a roll of his eyes.

I point my thumb towards the backseat. "But what if they don't love having another one? What if they're upset and mad and jealous? What if they grow up resenting the fact we threw another baby on them? And what if they start to resent *us*? What if they hate us for it?"

"They won't hate us."

He's using that tone, the one that suggests that I'm overreacting a tad bit. I dial it back a little. "I like the way things are. More babies would disrupt things."

"I just thought one–"

"You've seen pictures of my body–inside my body! Do you remember that internal ultrasound they made you watch, the one where you almost fainted? My insides are a perfect breeding ground for more than one baby! Look what happened before!"

"It doesn't mean it'll happen again. And I didn't almost faint."

"Sorry, that was the second one. I forgot."

I spend the rest of the drive to Emma and Cooper's going over my defense for not having another baby. There are many to choose from–the expense of more kids, my age, full house–but the truth is that I can't argue passionately about any of them. And I think J.B. knows it.

He knows I love kids. It's been my life's dream to be a mother, and it turns out I'm pretty good at it. Better than good. Another baby...

It doesn't mean I want to run out and get knocked up today, but it does mean that I can't find a good reason not to. I love kids, being pregnant. I love our life.

It scares me sometimes how good things are. I got my happily ever after, as unexpected as it was. Would having another baby put a damper on that?

I don't waste much time before I ask Cooper about it. J.B. may have known Cooper longer, but he's my best friend as much as he is J.B.'s. When we got to Cooper and Emma's, J.B. and Emma take the kids out to the backyard while I stay in the kitchen with Cooper.

"Did you know he wants to have another baby?" I ask Cooper. I can see the kids out the big window over the sink, chasing each other, with J.B. watching them with a smile on his face.

He's so happy being a dad. But is that a good enough reason to disrupt our life with more?

I'm gratified when Cooper flashes an expression of surprise. "J.B.? He hasn't said anything to me about a baby."

"Me neither. He threw it on me last night." I pluck a juicy strawberry out of the platter on the table. Emma is the perfect hostess. She always has kid-friendly food, as well as more adult fare, a neatly set table ready when we get there and always offers drinks before you need them. If we have people over, they're lucky if they get a handful of carrots for an appetizer, and I'm always passing out plates for a find-your-own seat type of meal.

Emma's outside with the kids now, teaching them how to use the bubble guns she got for them. Five of them, so there wouldn't be a problem with sharing. The kids may be great, but kids are kids and sharing is always a hard one to learn.

"It doesn't really surprise me." Cooper doesn't meet my gaze, but that could be because he's focused on the poached eggs. I love his eggs Benedict, which is why he usually makes them for us when we come for brunch. I always ask him how he can cook all week in the restaurant and still look so happy in his own kitchen, but he says that's just what he does. It's how he shows people he cares. It's like he's Italian.

"J.B.'s always talking about the kids," Cooper continues, whisking the hollandaise sauce. "And asking about mine. He's a different man since you had the trips, Casey. It's amazing to see."

"He's a great dad," I say. "That's not the issue."

"Are you trying to tell me *you* don't want another baby?" This time he meets my gaze with raised eyebrows of skepticism.

"I didn't say that."

"I wouldn't be surprised if you didn't." Cooper's always had a calming effect on me, but never has he been able to quiet my maelstrom of thoughts quicker than this. If Cooper thinks it's okay for me not to want another baby then it's really okay.

But then he continues. "Three is a lot to handle. Even if it was possible for Em and me, there's no way we'd add on the brood. And Emma is an amazing mother. But you, Casey, this is what you were made for. You've got such a talent with kids–your own and everyone else's. You show that being a teacher. You were made to be a mother."

I drop my head, unable to show him how touched I am by his words. "It doesn't feel like it some days."

"Trust me, if there's anyone who could handle your three and then more, it's you. And J.B. knows that. He probably thinks this is what you want."

"I'm pretty sure I never said the words *I want more kids* to him."

"Did you tell him the first time?"

"That was different."

Cooper shrugs, the exact same gesture J.B. used in the car. "Maybe it's preventative. He's throwing it out there before you can come out and tell him you're pregnant again."

"So you think he doesn't really want another one?" I grasp at the thought like a lifeboat floating away.

Cooper thrusts his chin towards the window. I glance out at the perfect moment where all five kids converge on a laughing J.B., sending him to his knees as they pelt him with bubbles from their bubble guns. "What do you think?"

I sigh.

"Two is enough for me and Em, but you two? You could have enough for a basketball team."

I widen my eyes in horror. "Do you think that's what he's doing? Making his own basketball team?"

Cooper laughs as he carefully lifts out a poached egg. "You have great kids, Casey. A few more wouldn't hurt."

"You say that now but wait until Sophie comes calling. She's told us she wants to live with you if we ever have to get rid of her."

I swear Cooper pales. "Sophie? Really? Not Ben? I'm better with boys. Or Lucy?"

***

Our last stop on Saturday is the grocery store. Sometimes if the kids are particularly active/whiny, J.B. will go himself, but I've found in recent years that all three love a good trip to the local Longos grocery store.

Today was no exception, especially when J.B. instigates a scavenger hunt, giving each kid three things to find. The rules are no leaving the store, don't eat anything, and stay out of the candy aisle.

You'd think shopping would be quick work with five of us collecting items off the weekly shopping list, but the game makes everything twice as long. Lucy is the first one to return with her mangoes, pound of butter and loaf of sourdough bread, but then she runs off to find Ben to see how he's making out, and then the two of them have to track down Sophie, who they find standing transfixed by the whole fish lying on a bed of ice still with head and tail intact.

When Sophie reports back, it's to tell us she's never eating fish again because they look alive with their eyeballs in.

"They're not alive," J.B. says patiently.

"But they do look alive." Lucy has a worried expression on her face. I suspect Sophie did her best to convince her the fish was indeed still breathing.

"They're really dead," J.B. assures them. "But not too dead or else they'd smell. Fish aren't supposed to smell."

"But they do when Momma cooks them," Ben points out.

"That was once because I burnt the fish sticks."

J.B. grimaces at the mention of the kids eating fish sticks. He has a horror of them, as well as chicken fingers and Kraft dinner.

"It's so easy to make your own," he always insists.

Maybe it is if you're a trained chef and have all the time in the world. But I don't comment as I push the cart towards the cashier line-ups.

Lucy gets to pick the line because she won the scavenger hunt. She helps me push the cart behind the one with the smiling baby waving at the kids.

I steal a glance at J.B. as we wait our turn. The three kids are mesmerized by the baby, a real cutie with a wisp of blond hair that makes it impossible to tell if it's a boy or girl. The green onesie doesn't help.

I guess a boy.

"What's his name?" Sophie demands of the mother. She tickles the baby's foot, while Ben plays peek-a-boo and Lucy constantly waves. The poor thing doesn't know where to look.

"It's a her," the mother tells Sophie. She's youngish, of the yoga-pants-and-UGGs species and still looks refreshed even in the middle of the afternoon.

Of course, she does–she only has one baby and there's a doting dad staring at his iPhone beside her.

"Her name is Sophie."

"That's *my* name," Sophie shrieks, loud enough for the whole store to hear. Baby Sophie laughs with delight at the outburst.

"It's a good name," the mother says. She glances at me, at my clothes that are wrinkled from bubble-soaked hugs from the kids and gives me a sympathetic smile. "Are they all yours? Sorry–they must be. All the hair."

I bristle at her tone, which isn't all that complimentary. "Yes, we've always been blessed with an abundance of hair." I stop myself from glancing down at her bald baby.

"Babies are so cute," Lucy sighs as the dad finally puts his phone away and starts loading the groceries on the belt.

I check out what they're buying. It's a little habit of mine. These folks are all-organic, vegetarian, and gluten-free. But not all gluten-free because there's a loaf of white Wonder bread tucked in there.

"Bye, baby Sophie," Sophie cries as the cart is pushed ahead to load the bags. My kids frantically wave at the baby, who smiles toothlessly back until the mother distracts her with a rice cracker.

"Aren't babies cute, Momma?" Lucy repeats.

"They are very cute," I say beginning to pile our selections because like the other dad, J.B. is also distracted by his phone. "The three of you were adorable."

"Yes, we were," Sophie agrees in all seriousness. "I've seen pictures. We were the *cutest*!"

"So if we had another baby, it would be the cutest too?" Lucy asks. She's helping me load, spreading boxes of granola bars haphazardly on the belt and making a pyramid of the crackers.

"Of course." A box of crackers drops to the floor and I bend to retrieve it.

When I stand, two sets of brown eyes and one of blue and hazel, are staring at me.

"We should have another baby," Lucy decides.

"Let's have another baby!" Sophie cheers.

"Can we have another baby?" Ben asks in all seriousness.

I glance at J.B., who appears as shocked by their requests as I am. Which is good, because if I find out that he set this up...

Chapter Seven

> Time away from the children should be carefully planned as to not disrupt the routine.
>
> *A Young Woman's Guide to Raising Obedient Children*
> Dr. Francine Pascal Reid, (1943)

The day is long and exhausting, with requests for more children–three more, says Sophie–and names for the new additions tossed around. When we get home, Lucy opens the file of baby pictures we have saved on my laptop. I've never gotten around to putting them in the baby books that still sit pristinely in their plastic wrapping on the shelf.

Someday.

J.B. escapes to the restaurant in the middle of this, giving me an unapologetic grin and leaving me with three minds fully focused on their potential new toy. They're like a dog with a bone–Baby! Baby! Baby!

"Kind of reminds me of you," J.B. says with a chuckle as the kids scramble to line up for hugs as he's leaving. "You were kind of fixated on the idea as well."

"I wanted to be a mother, not have something new to play with," I hiss, stepping out of the way as Sophie barrels back to the living room to gush at pictures of herself.

"Babies aren't a toy, Momma," Ben admonishes me.

"Of course not, Benny."

After J.B. leaves, the kids stare at the pictures for another hour before they get bored and move on to other activities. I go through our usual Saturday late afternoon routine of play and dinner which ends with us piled on the couch watching a movie before bed.

Tonight it's Sophie's choice–Disney's *Moana*. I let my mind drift as the kids sing along, Sophie reciting most of Maui's lines.

Having more kids... What would it be like? It would mean a return to the sleepless nights and diapers and feedings, but once the first few months were over, what would be so different? J.B. and I are outnumbered already, and the kids would love a baby. They were too young to remember Atticus and Aiden as babies, but I'm sure they would love another one.

They'd love it when it was cute and smiling, not crying with a distinct poopy smell.

When I was a surrogate for Cooper and Emma, I went into the experience with a firm thought and a cold heart. I was carrying *their* children. Not mine. And for the most part, I was able to disassociate myself from the living miracles I was carrying. I loved them, but not like I loved my kids.

But there were a few times when I lay awake at night, while the boys rolled and kicked, I wished they were mine. I wished I could wake J.B. and let him feel our babies kick because he missed out on a lot of it with the triplets. When I had been pregnant, he hadn't been lying beside me at night with his big hands cradling my belly, his eyes soft with love at the feel of little feet pushing at me.

When I decided to surrogate for Emma and Cooper, I had gone to my doctor to get checked out. She had been surprised but gave me a clean bill of health.

"You'll have to have another Caesarian, but there's no reason your body can't handle a few more kids," Dr. Morrissey had told me.

"Maybe not a few."

"Have you thought of adding to your brood?" she had asked. "You're doing something very special for your friends, but what about you? Want any more?"

I remember that day clearly because the kids had been two, and I had spent the night awake with Sophie and Lucy, Sophie throwing up, and Lucy crying, presumably because her sister was sick. I probably still smelled of sick when I went to the appointment.

"Not on your life," I had said firmly.

But now after one little comment from J.B., my carefully organized life with *no more kids* was in complete disarray, like a jigsaw puzzle dumped onto the table.

Did I want more kids?

I smoothed Lucy's hair and turned back to the movie, my eyes growing heavy as Moana and Maui battled the monsters from the deep.

"Casey."

I hear my name from a distance and blink my eyes open. J.B. is standing in front of me. It takes a few moments for me to realize that

I must have fallen asleep watching the movie because I'm not in bed, and there's a weight on my chest. Lucy. I can't see over her head to find out what—or who—the weight is on my legs.

"Hey." I swallow to rid the dryness of my mouth. The television is still on, with a list of Netflix recommendations.

"What were you watching?" J.B. gestures to the screen. Netflix is suggesting we might enjoy *Baywatch*. The last thing I'm interested in is a Dwayne Johnston marathon.

"*Moana*." I struggle to sit up. "But I'm a little stuck." After years of practice, we can speak quietly enough so the kids don't wake up.

"I can help you with that. You know you're missing a kid," J.B. says with a grin.

Instantly, I'm wide awake, ready to bolt upright. J.B. realizes what he's said. "Sorry. Sophie's in bed."

I exhale with a huff, and Lucy stirs. Her head is pillowed on my breasts, arms thrown out on either side of me.

"I can't get up without waking her," I whisper as Lucy's breathing returns to sleep mode.

"I have to move Ben first. He's down here."

By craning my head around Lucy's red curls, I see Ben's head propped up against Lucy's leg. "So cute."

J.B. lifts him carefully into his arms. "I'll be back for the next one."

My arms instinctively encircle Lucy as I wait. My nights often end with the kids in front of the TV: a little downtime for all of us. It's been a while since I've fallen asleep with them on the couch, though.

J.B. returns. "I put him in Sophie's bed because she's sleeping in his." He lifts Lucy off me, who grabs at me as she's airborne. "Daddy's got you," J.B. croons.

The girls share a room but more often than not, one of the girls will confiscate Ben's room, making him sleep with his other sister. There's never any fighting about it, and I think Ben likes the company.

I breathe deeply as her weight is lifted off me. There's a wet spot on my chest from Lucy's drool.

After turning off the TV and returning our empty popcorn bowl to the kitchen, I stop in the bathroom for a quick brush of my teeth before walking, zombie-like to our bedroom where J.B. is in the process of changing out of his work clothes.

My husband looks good in his slim-fitting pants that are just a little too tight around the bum, and a dark blue shirt and tie, but he looks even better when he's out of them. He doesn't work out as much as he used to, but weekly basketball games and bike riding with the kids, as well as being on his feet for long hours keeps him fit and trim and has delayed the inevitable middle-age paunch. I take a moment to appreciate the view.

Until he slips into a concert T-shirt long faded to gray and an old pair of boxer shorts with a rip along the seam.

Oh well.

"You looked cute on the couch like that," J.B. says over his shoulder with an affectionate smile. "I hated to wake you."

"I'm glad you did. That would have been a nasty way to wake up, with Lucy's face right in mine." I yawn without covering my mouth. "I need more sleep."

"Case."

His tone stops me as I'm about crawl into my side of the bed. "Do we have to do this now?"

"Do we have to do what?" He sits down on the edge and I take the opportunity to slip under the covers.

"Talk about the baby thing." Because I haven't been able to stop thinking about the possibility, and I'm not happy about it.

"How do you know that's what I want to talk about?"

I only look at him.

"Maybe I wanted to talk about how I think you should go to Las Vegas."

"You want me to go to Las Vegas?" I stare at him blankly until an image of Brit's face pops into my mind. "Vegas. Brit. Party. Right." My eyes close to half-mast as my head hits my memory foam cool comfort pillow. "Why would you want to talk about that? I've already told Brit I'm not going."

"I think it would do you good to go with her. Besides, she'll never forgive you if you miss it."

"Sometimes I wonder if that's a bad thing. No more Brit talking about herself." I heave a sigh as I roll over to face J.B. Maybe I should try to keep my eyes open for this conversation, as short as it's going to be.

"You'd have fun. And Morgan wants to go."

That got my attention. "How do you know that?"

"She texted me tonight, wondering how she could convince you to go."

"*Morgan* wants to go to Las Vegas?" Fully awake now, I sit upright. "And leave Carson behind?"

"Being a mom is tough, especially if you're doing it alone. Being a mom of three with a husband who's never around is even harder. I think you both need a break."

I narrow my eyes at him. "But you're going to have to stay home at night with the kids while I'm gone."

"Maybe I want to," J.B. says with an adorable sheepish grin on his face. "I miss out on a lot, and a couple of days of daddy time might be fun."

I don't bother to mask my laughter.

"I talked to Cooper tonight," J.B. continues, ignoring my derision. "He says it can work. We're training Miles as assistant manager, and it'll be a good test for him to be on his own for a weekend. We thought maybe Tenley could come work for Saturday in case there's any problems. It's only for a couple of days, right?"

"Brit wants to leave Thursday, come home Sunday night."

"I can do that." He meets my incredulous gaze. "I can."

"I know you can." I relent with a soft sigh. "And it's not that I don't think you could. It's just that..."I glance down at my hands kneading the blanket. "I think I feel guilty. Thinking about how I kind of want to go makes me feel horrible! How could I want to leave the kids? They're all I wanted for so long and to think getting on a plane without them–"

J.B.'s laughter stops my rant. "It's not bad that you want to go away with your friends. You're with the kids all the time. A break will do you good."

"But it's *away*."

"Away can be good because you'd come back. It's not like it's forever."

"What if it is?" I whisper, giving voice to my deepest fear. "What if something happens?"

He reaches across the bed for me. "You're nuts," he whispers as his strong arms wrap around me.

"But things happen," I persist. "Things happen in Las Vegas."

"Don't even go there." His voice is strong and sure and reassuring. "You're not one to live your life in fear. Go and celebrate Brit. Drink a lot, stay away from good-looking men and have fun."

"What about not good-looking men?" I ask as I pull away.

"What would you want with an ugly man in Vegas when you can have a good-looking man here?"

I shrug. "Fair point. Are you sure?"

"Do you want me to pack for you?"

"You wouldn't have a clue how to begin." I kiss him, my lips lingering against his. "You're good for me."

"I know. Sorry to bring up the baby thing now. Try not to think about it now. There's no rush. We can talk about it when you're back."

"There's no rush?" I flop back onto the pillows and recite from memory. "A woman's prime period of fertility occurs between the years of twenty-two and twenty-eight, with each year decreasing the chance of a happy and healthy conception."

J.B. grimaces. "Is that from that book you were reading when you got pregnant?"

I nod. "A Young Woman's Guide to the Joy of Impending Motherhood. She wrote another one." I show him the dog-eared book on my nightstand, A Young Woman's Guide to Raising Obedient Children.

J.B. bursts out laughing. "A lot of good that book has been."

Chapter Eight

> Friendships with other mothers should be cultivated to ensure a proper network of support.
>
> *A Young Woman's Guide to Raising Obedient Children*
> Dr. Francine Pascal Reid, (1943)

Brit is smug when I tell her I can go to Las Vegas with her. "I knew you'd come around," she chortles. "Morgan told me yesterday that she was in, and I was just waiting for you to come to your senses."

"The logistics took some work," I admit.

"We'll have a fabulous time!" The excitement in Brit's voice is sincere. This might be her fourth wedding, but it's been a while since we've gone away together.

There's a lot of history between Brit and me, and a lot of traveling. Including the infamous European trip after graduation that led me to break up with the then love of my life, David Mason.

Who had been *thisclose* to being the father of my baby, if J.B. hadn't gotten me pregnant. And if David hadn't turned out to be gay.

But that's another story.

Agreeing to the trip was the easy part. Planning things is much more difficult. Brit takes care of finding flights and hotels, emailing me a long list of names and numbers that I spend the next few evenings booking and confirming. But it's the stuff at home that keeps me up at night worrying about. Like leaving detailed instructions for J.B. about pickups and playdates and soccer games. I double-check everything with my sister Libby, who is on call for emergencies. Not that I don't think J.B. will be able to make it, but he needs to have a backup in case he has a crisis at work. I know the kids come first, but *Thrice* is like another child to him.

Then why does he want another baby? Why not just open another restaurant?

As much as I want to stop thinking about having another baby, I just can't. When I have something on my mind, I can't let it go until it's resolved. Before I got pregnant, it was my only focus for a few weeks. Baby. Baby. Baby.

Cooper used to call me obsessive.

What if I decide I really don't want a baby, but J.B. does? What if I want it, but he changes his mind halfway through? Or when I'm about to deliver and he gets cold feet–

J.B. would never do that.

I have to stop thinking about this. My babies are tucked in their beds, with visions of soccer games in their heads.

I'll miss their soccer game.

I sigh and check the schedule Brit has emailed me. We leave in three days, and Brit is a bundle of organizational nerves. Now *she* is more than a bit obsessive when planning for her weddings. Why she thinks she needs a stagette for her fourth wedding, I'll never know. She's already had three legendary bachelorette parties, as well as a couple of pretty good divorce parties.

Why does she need to be married for a fourth time? If you mess up three times, I think you'd give up. And it's not like Brit is a sucker for romance. I've only met her fiancé, Justin, once, and he certainly didn't give me the warm and fuzzies. Nice enough, but I wouldn't be racing down the aisle to marry him.

But I've long figured out that Brit gets more satisfaction in planning the weddings and everything that goes along with it. She should have gone into event planning rather than finance. When we were teenagers thinking about the future, my focus would be on babies, Brit's on planning her weddings. Weddings–plural. She rarely talked about husbands, other than whether it would be a good idea to marry one of the Backstreet Boys or should she hold out for Leonardo Dicaprio.

Looking at how the careers panned out, I think Leo would have been the better bet.

Even so, four weddings are a lot of weddings. Maybe she's trying to one-up me–I have three kids, she's had four husbands. Brit's always had a competitive side so I wouldn't put it past her. Whatever makes her happy.

I've come to the conclusion a long time ago that there are few things in Brit's life that truly make her happy.

And after I look at her schedule and check my confirmations, I realize I'm not going to be one of them.

I take a deep breath and pick up the phone.

"So when is your flight?" I ask hesitantly after Brit says hello.

"In three days," Brit says, exasperation evident in her voice as if she's gone through this with me countless times. She hasn't, since it's the first time I've glanced at her schedule. "The car will pick you up at three-thirty, which will get you to the airport and through security in time to have a drink before our flight."

"And that's at si— fifteen?"

"What's the problem, Casey?" The exasperation has changed to iciness. "Please don't tell me there's a championship soccer game you can't miss."

"There actually is a soccer game, but that's not it. I think I'll have trouble getting that flight. I think maybe if you told me your flight was eighteen-fifteen–"

"What the hell is eighteen-fifteen?"

"Six-fifteen pm. It's the military time, the time that airlines follow. You said 6:15 so I booked the six-fifteen flight."

"In the morning?" Brit's voice screeches from cell tower to cell tower, finally arriving in my ear, still in full-fright mode.

"That's what time you said."

"No, our flight is six-fifteen. *PM.*"

"You didn't tell me that."

"I was fairly certain that I did."

"You should have said eighteen-fifteen. Or six-fifteen pm."

The argument between Brit and I goes on for quite some time, with Brit demanding that I change the flight. I'm sure it would be easy enough to do, but it's the principle of the thing. She should have told me the right time for the flight.

In the end, J.B. convinces me to keep the flight the way it is.

"Go early, check into the room, and then go sit by the pool. Or go shopping. This trip is supposed to be a break for you, and God knows you'll need to rest up before you have forty-eight hours with Brit."

"I think it's more like sixty," I say nervously.

CHAPTER NINE

> Dreaming of your children hurt or injured is a minor occurrence and should be disregarded as a mother's subconsciousness cannot be trusted.
>
> *A Young Woman's Guide to Raising Obedient Children*
> Dr. Francine Pascal Reid, (1943)

Since I have to be at the airport at such an ungodly hour, I say goodbye to the kids the night before I leave. Lugging my suitcase behind me, I try and make it out of the room without waking J.B., but accidentally slam it into the dresser on the way to the door.

His sharp intake tells me I've failed in my attempt not to wake him. "Casey?"

"Sorry," I whisper. "I didn't want to wake you. Go back to sleep."

He sits up, his hair mussed from sleep. "Were you going without saying goodbye?"

"There was a goodbye last night. It was long, and there were tears. If I do that again, I don't think I'll be able to leave."

A chuckle from the bed. "Get over here."

Like I can say no to that. I crawl onto the bed beside him and let him wrap me in his arms, breathing in the sleep smell of him. He still smells good, other than his breath. I try not to breathe through my nose.

"We'll be fine here," he assures me.

"I know."

"And you'll have a good time."

"Okay."

"Have you called for an Uber yet?"

"When I get my stuff downstairs."

J.B. shifts and pulls away. Already I miss him. "I'll help you, or you might wake everyone up."

"It was only a little bang." I pick up my big Coach purse that works as a carry-on bag and let J.B. carry my suitcase down the stairs.

I pause outside the kids' doors. Last night all three insisted on sleeping in the same room, with Ben on a makeshift bed on the floor. The tears threaten again as I give the door a little wave.

J.B. waits at the door with me until I see the headlights of the car. I notice how dark it is outside. I used to love getting up at this time of the night to feed the kids. It was always so quiet, without the cars or buses. I always felt like I was the only one in the city awake.

"It's always darkest just before dawn," I say to J.B., quoting an old Laura Ingalls Wilder saying.

"Have fun in the dark, then," J.B. says, wrapping me in a hug.

"Be careful with the kids." My voice is muffled against his chest.

"What am I going to do, break them?"

"Please don't."

I'm already close to tears at the thought of being away from them for four days. Thinking of them broken in some way just about puts me over the edge.

"I won't break your kids," he assures me.

"They're your kids too."

"Which is why I am perfectly capable of taking care of them. You think so too. You told me that."

"Maybe I had been drinking when I said that," I say in a small voice.

"Casey." He tips my chin up. "Everything will be fine."

"You know what fine stands for, don't you? Fucked up, insecure, neurotic–"

"Casey!" His tone of exasperation stops me.

"Everything will be fine," I echo. "I'll have fun."

"You will have fun. Say hi to the girls. I love you."

"Love you too." We kiss as the headlights flash impatiently against the window. "I better go."

J.B. opens the door for me and carries my suitcase to the car. "Try to stay out of the trouble," he says as leans down for one last kiss.

"I'll do my best." Hopefully, the forced wink distracts him from my quivering chin. "But I'm not promising."

I wave as the car drives away, and keep waving even after J.B. goes back into the house. I take a deep breath, and then another. It's fine. I'm fine. It's only four days.

"Early flight?" the Uber driver asks.

"I'm going to Las Vegas."

"The city that never sleeps. You'll fit right in."

I hide a yawn. "I think I'll need a nap."

As I drive away from the house, the enormity of what I'm doing hits me. I've rarely been away from the kids for more than a few hours. I'm a full-time kindergarten teacher, but when the kids were in daycare, they were so close that five minutes after the school bell rang, I was picking them up. They spent an overnight at my sister's, and the odd afternoon with Cooper and Emma, but that's it.

The kids are my life, and I'm going away without them.

But as much as I love them, I love myself too. And I love Morgan and Brit. J.B. was right to push me into this. I need something else in my life because someday my kids are going to be gone. They're going to move out, be far away from me...

I clamp my hands over my mouth to stifle the whimper.

I obviously didn't get enough sleep last night if I'm getting upset over something that may or may not happen in twelve years' time.

If we were to have another baby now, the kids will be seven when the new baby arrives. Is that too big a gap? And I'll be forty-three–is that too old to be the mother of a newborn?

I don't feel like a forty-year-old. Despite the constant exhaustion, the more time I spend with the kids, the younger I feel. Maybe having a baby would be a good thing.

How old would I be when a baby becomes a teenager? Has J.B. even thought of that?

The lack of traffic snarls and construction backups at four am makes it a speedy drive to the airport. I try not to think about J.B. back in bed as I wheel my bag into the airport.

The last time I traveled by myself was a few years before the kids came along. Brit and I decided to go to Paris for a few days. Before that was Cuba and Mexico. I've been to Europe three times. I am a world-class traveler, so what is the knot of anxiety tightening in my stomach?

The kids will be fine, I repeat as I march up to the counter.

And so will I.

Despite the Starbucks latte and the Tim Horton's donut and wasting some time wandering the few shops open at this hour, and riding twice on the moving sidewalk, the early hour gets to me, and I end up in the boarding area, slumped uncomfortably in a chair, fighting off sleep.

"Boarding Flight 741 at Gate D."

My eyes fly open. "What...Where..." I look around wildly, with no idea where I am.

"The plane's getting ready to board," says a man sitting beside me.

Airport. The chairs had been nearly empty when I had sat down, but now they are chockablock, with strangers staring at me. Especially the kindly-faced older man next to me. I try to calm my heart rate but then–

"Where are the kids?"

The man's kindly face turns confused. "What kids?"

"*My* kids!" I jump to my feet, the book flying off my lap. "Where–?"

"You had children with you?" He stares at me in shock. "I didn't see anyone with you!"

"My kids, they're..." I trail off, heaving a deep breath as I finally comprehend where I am. Airport. Vegas. Brit. Standing in the middle of the waiting area looking foolish. I sit down quickly. "They're at home."

"Are you sure?" he booms.

"I'm sorry." Hand on my heart, I turn to him, to see the look of fear mirrored on his face. "I'm so sorry, but I was just confused."

He lets out a whoosh of coffee-scented breath and slumps back into his seat. "You can't do that to a man. I don't think my heart could take it."

"I'm sorry," I repeat. "I didn't mean to fall asleep."

"Harold?" A woman walks over to us, her hands full of Tom Horton's cups. "What's going on?" She frowns at me as she hands Harold his coffee.

"I was a bit confused when I woke up," I apologize. "I thought I lost my kids, but they're not even here."

"Where are they?" Harold asks. He has a nice voice, deep and kind, like his eyes. I notice they're wearing matching khaki pants and brightly coloured shirts. Retirees leaving for vacation.

I take another deep breath. "Back home with my husband. Hopefully still in bed." I stoop to pick up my book, collect my purse from under the chair. "I'm really sorry if I freaked you out."

"As long as they're safe," Harold says, hugging his coffee to his chest like it might calm him. What I must have done to his poor heart.

His wife sits beside him and leans around to face me. "I used to wake up in the middle of the night thinking the baby was somewhere in the bed," she says. "It so upset my husband."

I glance from her to him. "Then you must be used to it."

"Oh, I wasn't married to him," she says dismissively. "Still not."

"Oh, I thought–you're not–" I stammer.

"Oh no," she trills before turning doting eyes at Harold. "Well, maybe someday."

Harold, honest to goodness, blushes a deep red.

"She doesn't need to hear any of that, Winnie," he mutters.

Winnie gives a girlish giggle.

My face breaks into a smile. "I think I maybe do. Now that my heart's started beating again."

"Not a nice thing to do; joke about heart attacks with a couple who are on the danger list."

I feel my face fall. "Uh...sorry."

She looks up with a twinkle in her eye. "Just joking. We've got at least twenty minutes before the flight boards and you can tell us all about your kids and husband who is letting you jet off all by yourself."

J.B. I pull out my phone. "I just need to..." I mutter, my thumbs tapping furiously.

I know it's early and you've gone back to bed but
PLEASE text me that kids are ok. Fell asleep in airport and dreamed I lost them.

Either he hasn't gone back to sleep or the chime of the phone wakes him up because he replies right away.

Kids are still where you left them last night.
Checking now...1,2, and 3. All good. Going back to sleep.
Thank you. Love you.

He sends me a kissy face emoji in return.

"Kids are fine," I report to Harold as I put my phone away. "It's just me I have to worry about."

Chapter Ten

> Automobiles are not an advisable mode of transportation for children.
>
> *A Young Woman's Guide to Raising Obedient Children*
> Dr. Francine Pascal Reid, (1943)

I haven't been on a plane since last year when we took the kids to Disneyland. That had been a bit of an adventure. J.B. got pulled out of line and searched for drugs, Sophie threw up while we were waiting in line to check in and Lucy and Ben both threw up during the flight–several times–with Sophie crying *for* them, because neither of them could keep their heads out of the air sickness bags.

I remember how the rest of the passengers had let us off the plane first. I heard the collective sigh of relief as we carried the kids off. I didn't let myself cry then, even though I really wanted to.

But as the plane levels off, leaving the early morning lights of Toronto behind, I have to admit I shed a few tears. A few days away *will* be a good thing for me. The kids *will* be all right with J.B. They'll have a great time with him. And a few days away from *all* my kids–not only my own but my kindergarten class–will help. I love being a teacher, but a couple of days to recharge my batteries is exactly what the doctor ordered.

I see the back of Harold's head a few rows ahead of me and smile at the memory of the shock on his face. That gets rid of the tears.

*

The five-hour flight literally flies by. I catch a quick nap, the movie is one I haven't seen and my seatmates are just the right amount of chatty, telling me about their previous trips to Las Vegas and things to do. The flight attendants keep the coffee coming. By the time I step out of the airport, I'm full of excitement and caffeine.

In the taxi, my eyes practically bug out of my head when I catch sight of the legendary Strip. Las Vegas–I'd seen pictures but never imagined it would be like *this*. Barely eight am on a Thursday morning and already the sidewalks are as congested as the streets of Toronto during the Friday afternoon exodus to cottage country.

"Oh my god," I breathe, loud enough for the cab driver to hear.

"First time here?" he asks.

"How can you tell?" I laugh, unable to stop gazing out the window. The morning sun dims the lights from the hotels, but it's still dazzling to my eyes.

I pull out my phone again, taking a video of the people, the cars, *everything* and send it to J.B. to show the kids. I take in as much as I can before the taxi drops me in front of the Cosmopolitan Hotel and Resort.

Slowly the heavy weight of leaving the kids is disappearing.

"Have fun!" the driver calls before I slam the door behind me.

As I cross the marble floor of the lobby, heading to the concierge desk, I realize I must look like the kids did when they first saw the characters at Disney. Sophie squealed with excitement as she hugged Tigger; Ben's eyes were huge with awe as Mickey shook his hand, and Lucy hid behind me, afraid to go near the Little Mermaid.

I have a mixture of all of those emotions.

"Good morning," the girl at the desk sings as I stop before the desk. "Welcome to the Cosmopolitan Hotel and Resort."

She's a perky one. But I fix the smile on my face even though perky people often make me cringe, especially early in the morning. "Hi. I just got here from Toronto. I'm meeting my friends later, but I got an earlier flight–" I stop myself before I give the girl the full story. "When would I be able to check in?"

Perky or not, Ashleigh is helpful, promising me I can get into my room by eleven thirty rather than the usual three o'clock, and stores my bags for me.

And then I head out to the Strip, feeling exhilarated as I merge into the packed sidewalk with a need to see everything.

For the first time, I'm glad I left the kids at home because I'd be petrified that I'd lose them in the crowd.

I walk the length of The Strip, hitting ten thousand steps on my Fitbit in no time. I find Circus Circus at the north end, lingering outside as I think how much fun the kids would have in Adventuredome, the indoor park.

I shop, picking up a bag of souvenirs for the kids, including a toy slot machine that shoots out candy instead of quarters. I find purple-and-yellow scarves for Brit and Morgan, cheap and tacky but a perfect memento of our weekend together. I stop for more coffee and swap my heeled boots that I didn't want to pack for a pair of cute red TOMS so my feet won't rebel.

For the first time in six years, I have fun being by myself. The kids are fine, and even though they pop into my mind at regular intervals, I don't worry. There's no one calling my name, trailing me to the bathroom; there's no need to ask if anyone needs a washroom or a snack. I stop when I have to pee or if I'm hungry.

This is freedom for a mother and I enjoy it.

But I tire after a few hours and head back to the Cosmopolitan.

Brit booked us a two-room suite, with king-size beds and a terrace with a view of the Bellagio fountains. I spend long minutes hanging over the railing and watching the water rise and fall before I explore the place.

The bathroom alone is huge, with a Japanese soaking tub and a rain shower stall, thick towels and the softest toilet paper I've ever experienced. The minibar is stocked full of drinks, snacks and countless tiny bottles of alcohol and wine–

And the bed…

The bed looks like an island paradise after being shipwrecked. I don't take off my shoes before I take a running leap. Then I get up and strip off my shoes and pants and shirt and crawl back under the covers. It feels like I've been up for an entire day.

I do the calculations in my head. I've been awake long enough for a nap. In no time at all, I drift off to sleep, nestled among the cool sheets and fluffy duvet.

The nap was nice, but what isn't nice is that I forget to turn down my phone. The insistent sound of a baby crying yanks me out of sleep.

The kids are crying!

And then I realize it's just my phone and the stupid ring tone J.B. put on, knowing that the sound of a baby crying would instantly get my attention, no matter what I was doing.

I find it on the bed beside me. "Hello?"

"GOOOAAALLL!"

My eyes blink open at the chorus of little voices. "Hello?" I ask, my voice still sleep-clogged.

"Momma, Benny got a goal! A GOAL!" It's Sophie's little voice, yelling to be heard over Lucy and Ben's.

"He got a goal?"

"His first goal ever and I helped him! I set it up perfectly and he kicked it in and it looked like the goaltender was going to stop it, but he didn't and Benny scored!"

It warms my heart that Sophie is more excited for her brother than she had been when she got her first goal last year. Then my heart breaks when I realize Ben got a milestone and I wasn't there to see it.

"That's so great!" I heap every ounce of enthusiasm into my tone; hopefully, Sophie won't hear the sleepiness in my voice or sense the fat tears filling my eyes.

"Here's Benny." Distant voices and then Sophie's strident tone. "Just put her on speaker!"

"Ben?"

"Hi, Momma!"

"I'm so proud of you, sweetie! Your first goal. So great!"

By the time I've spoken to the three of them and got the highlights of the soccer game repeated several times, I've managed to wake up enough to mask the tears in my voice.

I missed his first goal.

"Are you having fun, Momma?" Ben asks finally. "Have you seen Elvis yet? Daddy told us the place is full of Elvises and quarters falling on the ground."

"Pick up the quarters for us, Momma!" Lucy cries in the background.

"I will," I promise, fighting back the tears. "All the quarters I find. And I'll take a picture of Elvis for you, Ben." How do they even know who Elvis is? What's J.B. been telling them?

I finally hear J.B.'s voice over the kids'. "Say bye to Momma now, and go get your snack before it's all gone," he orders.

"Bye Momma!" they chorus.

"Have lots and lots and lots of fun," Lucy chimes in.

"Don't miss us too much because we're good with Daddy," Ben assures me.

"But miss us enough to come home," Sophie adds.

And then they're gone, their little voices disappearing into the distance. I picture them running off to join the throng around whatever parent had brought snacks that week.

It was Lisa so it'd be a good snack for them.

"Casey?"

"Take me off speakerphone," I beg.

"How's it going? Are you having fun?"

"No, I'm not having fun!" I burst. "You made me come here, and Ben scored his first goal and I missed it. Did you get a picture? A video of it."

"Nita got a video of the whole game. I'll get it from her. It was a great shot, Case; you'd be proud of him."

"Of course I'm proud of him! I want to be there to see it, not here in a hotel room with a really comfortable bed."

"Are you crying?"

"No!" But the sob escapes in a laugh/cough sound.

"There'll be other goals," J.B. assures me, sounding so tender that I have to choke back another sob.

"He's been playing for two years and this is the first! What if it's the only one? And I missed it because I took a selfish trip away from them. I want to come home."

"Casey..."

"I mean it. I'm going to get the first flight home. With the time difference, I think I can make it before they go to bed."

"Stop it, Casey. You're there to have fun. There'll be other games. The kids are fine. You need this."

"I need to be with them."

"You need some time with your friends. If you try to book another flight, I'm canceling your credit card."

"You're what?"

"You're not coming home early. Stay. Have fun. What time do Brit and Morgan get in?"

"Soon." I glance at the clock radio on the bedside table. I slept for almost three hours. Brit and Morgan's flight will get in at six.

"You should go meet them at the airport. Take them a big drink."

"I don't think I can take alcohol through the airport," I sniff.

"This is Brit's party, and hopefully her last one. Make it fun for her. If you sit around missing the kids, you'll never hear the end of it."

"Maybe," I sulk.

"She's your oldest friend, and she's getting married. Don't be sad, Case. You're there–have fun. Have a great time."

"I can't."

"You can, and you will. Promise me no more pity party?" When I don't answer, his voice grows louder. "Promise me you'll have fun!"

"I promise," I reluctantly say.

"I love you."

"I hate you for making me come here," I growl. "But I love you too."

CHAPTER ELEVEN

> Expect all manner of changes after becoming a mother—physical, psychological and social. Your world has adjusted and you must change with it.
>
> *A Young Woman's Guide to Raising Obedient Children*
> Dr. Francine Pascal Reid, (1943)

I decide to take J.B.'s advice to meet the girls at the airport because even though I hate to admit it at times, he's a pretty smart guy. Brit will appreciate me making the effort to go to her, rather than waiting in the room with a bottle of champagne, which was what I had been planning to do.

It would be easy to sit here and wallow in self-pity, missing them all, but I promised J.B. I wouldn't do that. The kids want me to have fun too.

"I'm here to have fun, so fun I shall have," I tell my reflection in the mirror before I head to the bathroom.

I take a moment to contemplate how much fun J.B. and I could have in the room before stripping off to stand under the rainforest showerhead.

The soothing water manages to wake me up and wipe away the remnants of my tears. And once I finish my shower, clad only in a thick white towel, I call room service for some champagne.

Brit expects a bottle to be waiting for her, and I would be a bad friend if I didn't taste test it for her.

Thank goodness for the alcohol, because I soon find that getting ready to go out with the girls in Sin City is like hauling myself up a huge hill.

I used to do this. I used to be very social, with dates, and parties and big groups of friends. Drinking, dancing, meeting new people.

But when was the last time I went to a party that didn't involve kids? And where the hosts provided adult beverages rather than organic juice boxes? Since I've had the kids, my social life has taken a nosedive. And my friendships have, well, dwindled to Morgan and Brit and other couples with kids.

J.B. will still ask me occasionally if I want to go out on one of his nights off. But I know he likes to spend that time with the kids, and honestly, it makes me tired to think about the effort it takes to go out. Finding babysitters, not to mention what it takes me to get ready these days.

Is that what happens when you become parents, or when you get older? Because I've noticed Brit's social calendar is more open than it used to be five years ago. Of course, this could be because Brit is sometimes not a nice person.

I shouldn't think that. Brit is my oldest and dearest friend. We've been together through all my mother's shenanigans, her parent's divorce, all of her divorces, my dating disasters, the babies. We've been through a lot and no matter what I may think of her at times, I'm still proud to be her maid of honor.

Matron of honor now. That's another thing that's changed.

I'll do my best to dip my toe into the Fountain of Youth tonight. I don't know if it's being here in Las Vegas or J.B.'s many lectures about having fun, but I take the preparations for this evening seriously.

The music turns on and I dance around the bathroom. The kids and I still have dance parties in the kitchen. I smile at the thought of Ben's serious man-moves, of Sophie twirling and spinning until she makes herself so dizzy that she falls over. Of Lucy's uncoordinated limbs that always makes me vow to enroll her in a dance class.

The makeup comes out, and I shadow and blend like a pro. The unruly curls are straightened into a red sheet down my back.

Holy shit, is that a white hair? In my eyebrow?

I tug at the offending hair with my fingers. Did I not bring a pair of tweezers? How could I I leave home without some? What if I got a sliver...or found a goddam white hair in my eyebrow?

I'm not that old, am I? Why am I thinking of having a baby if I have white hairs?

I snatch up the phone in the room and connect to the front desk. "Cosmopolitan Hotel and Resort. We're here to serve your every need so how can I help you?" It's a perky female voice and I wonder if it's Ashleigh from earlier.

"I need a pair of tweezers?"

"Pardon me?"

"This is Casey Samms-Bergen in room– "

"Yes, Ms. Samms-Bergen, how can I help you?"

"I need to borrow a pair of tweezers. Or buy them, I guess. Can you help me with that?"'

A pause. "Do you have a sliver? Do you need a doctor?"

"No, I...You're a woman, right? Look, I just found my first white hair and I really need to get rid of it. Like now, because once my friend gets here she's going to notice it right away and–"

"I can help you with that, Ms. Samms-Bergen." Whoever she is, the girl has lost her perky tone and exchanged it for one that's close to pitying.

I sigh. "Since we're talking personal hygiene, I guess you can call me Casey."

They send someone up with a brand new pair of tweezers still in the packaging. I have no doubt I'll see it on the bill, but it's worth it as I attack the invading hair. Once I finish my preparations, I preen in front of the mirror for a few minutes.

I may be the mother of three children, but I've still got it. I've also got the extra ten pounds of baby weight that I've never been able to get rid of, but I hide it under the loose, flowing shirt that leaves my shoulders bare.

And my backside still looks good in my tight black pants.

I arrange to have a taxi waiting to take me to the airport, but after I get ready, I have enough time to wander around the casino before it's time to leave. When I headed to the room earlier, I bypassed it entirely, my head pounding from lack of sleep, my heart heavy from missing the kids. But I feel better now, and with my new *have fun* resolutions, I want to see as many things to tell the kids about.

Plus, it'd be fun to find a couple of quarters rolling around to bring home to Sophie.

The lights and the noise of the casino threaten to overwhelm me–it's spastic, hypnotic, with no rhyme nor reason. But it also sucks me in and after a trip around the tables, admiring the clothes, the confident players showing absolutely no emotion, I find myself in front of one of the one-arm bandits with a handful of quarters rattling in my purse.

I can't not play. Only a couple of times. The taxi will be here in a half-hour; I can play for a few minutes and still have time to get a drink at the bar.

Twenty-two minutes later, I'm still there and down to my last few quarters.

"This is my last time," I mutter as I feed the coin into the slot. Nothing. "This is my very last time."

I pull the bar, glancing at the middle-aged man beside me. He's been there longer than I have, feeding coins in with a ferocity that's more than a little frightening.

An alarm blasts, lights flash, and for a moment I think he's won.

"You won," he tells me with less emotion than the poker players.

"Holy shit!" Coins begin pouring out of the machine. The lights, the alarm, the noise of the quarters is awesome, and I stand staring at the slot machine. "I think I won. I won! I never win anything!"

And once again, I pull out my phone, taking pictures of the coins overflowing onto the floor. The man beside me looks at me with disgust.

"Are you just going to leave them there?"

For a moment, I think he's going to take my winnings, and frantically begin stuffing quarters into my purse, my pockets...some even go into my bra. I glance over my shoulder, feeling the staring, unable to stop the grin.

If Sophie was here, she would be racing around to pick up every last coin. And Ben would follow her, his hands open to hold them for his sister. Lucy would be cheering...

I wish they were here to see this.

"I found a few for you," a deep voice behind me says. Still crouched on the floor, I look up, way up. He's tall, he's built, and he's very bald. And he's holding a handful of quarters.

"Thank you." I stumble to my feet, my hands full and useless. I look at him helplessly and laugh. "I don't know where to put them all."

"You can exchange them over there." He nods to a wicket in the corner of the casino.

I stuff the coins in my hands in my purse, which is already overflowing. "I don't have time," I admit. "I have to pick up my girls at the airport."

"Your girls? Like, kids?"

"Girlfriends," I correct. "My kids are at home. Two girls and a boy." I give my head a shake. "You don't want to know that. I'm here for a stagette."

He smiles knowingly still holding a handful of my winnings. I have never seen broader shoulders on a man. He's about the size of a tree, with arms the size of my legs. "You keep them," I say impulsively. "Thanks for being a nice guy and not stealing them."

"Are you staying at the hotel?" he asks. I nod. "I'll find you later. Here." He drops the handful of quarters in his pocket before handing me a colourful flyer.

"I can't...You want to sell me something?" I stammer, clutching my oversize purse with two hands, so he reaches around and tucks it into the back pocket of my pants with a rueful smile.

"Sorry to be so forward. It's for a show tomorrow night. Bring your friends. And have fun."

I stare at him, mouth open as he walks away. Then with a last glance at the floor to check for runaway coins, I turn and race to the front doors, only to find my cab ready to leave without me.

UNEXPECTINGLY HAPPILY EVER AFTER

"Wait, please," I cry, my hands full so it takes a moment to open the door. "I need to get to the airport." Coins fall out of my purse as I throw myself in the car. "Thanks."

The driver turns and glares at me over his shoulder. "Is someone going to be chasing us for that money? Because I charge extra for that."

"What? No, this is mine. I won it–"

"Why in such a hurry then? Going to the airport with no bags? Suspicious, wouldn't you say?"

My mouth falls open. The last ten minutes have been plenty unbelievable, but this? "Uh, I had a few minutes before I had to leave. I'm meeting my friends at the airport, not leaving. I just got here this morning, so even though I miss my kids, I'm not ready to go home."

The realization surprises me.

"And I was playing the slots and all this money came out because I won but I didn't have time to cash it in because Brit and Morgan's flight gets in..." I glance at my Fitbit. "Like now. So can we go? To the airport, so I can meet them? Not run away?"

The driver turns. "Fair enough." Without another word, he pulls away from the hotel, leaving me staring after him.

Did he just accuse me of stealing the money?

I spend the twenty minutes rearranging my purse so the coins fit, without another word to the driver. He doesn't get a very good tip.

In the airport, it's easy to find the line of burly guys in chauffeur uniforms holding up signs. Brit mentioned she'd have a car waiting, but I never expected this. It's just like in a movie. The driver for Brit is on the end. "That's not for the real Britney Spears, is it?" I ask worriedly, gesturing to the sign that says, Ms. Spears.

There's a small group behind the chauffeurs, tittering excitedly.

Brit's full moniker, including married names, is Britney Annabeth Spears Smith Dover Hart, but she still goes by Brit Spears. Since then, she's had a hate on the singer, even refusing to talk to me for a day when I casually mentioned that I would have liked to have seen her show in Vegas.

It's too bad. I like her music.

"I don't know if she's real or not," the chauffeur says with a bored expression. "I'm only supposed to hold the sign."

But then I see Brit and Morgan walking towards us, talking and laughing. I push down the FOMO feeling that I should have changed my flight to be with them, and rush towards them from behind the line of chauffeurs.

"Casey!" Brit cries. "You're here!"

She looks so happy to see me.

"Welcome to Las Vegas and the best weekend of your life!" I shriek.

Chapter Twelve

> Mothers should be often reminded that there are subjects other than their children that should be used in conversation.
>
> *A Young Woman's Guide to Raising Obedient Children*
> Dr. Francine Pascal Reid, (1943)

"This place is amazing," Morgan sighs as she sinks onto the bed we're sharing. Because this is Brit's weekend, she gets the bedroom to herself. "I'm jealous that you got time here by yourself."

"J.B. convinced me. He said time by myself would be good, and he was right."

Morgan grimaces. "I hate to admit it, but isn't he usually?"

"Yes," I mimic Morgan's sigh. "It's annoying."

"Kids are okay with him?"

"Loving it." Quickly I tell her about Ben's goal. Brit is in the bathroom, showering off the "flight smell" before our evening out so Morgan and I are able to talk about the kids without her freaking out.

Brit has already told us twice that there is to be no "kid-talk" this weekend.

"Yay, Benny. But Casey, this is exactly what I was afraid of. Carson is going to start talking and I'm going to miss it. I've already texted my mother four times since the plane got in."

"Without Brit noticing?"

Morgan grins. "I'm very sneaky about it."

With perfect timing, my cell chimes an incoming FaceTime call. "You can't be sneaky with that ringtone," Morgan laughs as I fumble for my phone.

"Hi, babe." J.B.'s smiling face greets me. "Is this a bad time?"

"No, it's perfect." I glance over my shoulder. Hopefully, Brit will be in the shower for a few more minutes.

"The kids wanted to say goodnight." Instantly his face is replaced by my little angels squashed together with each trying to get the most screen time.

"Goodnight, Momma!" Sophie cries. She's holding the phone, but only half of her face is showing. Ben and Lucy hover over her shoulders. "I love you!"

"I love you, Momma," Ben says. His eyes widen with excitement. "I got a goal."

"I know," I smile, blinking back the tears that threaten at the sight of their faces. "I'm so proud of you."

"I didn't hit anyone this time," Sophie chimes in. "But I wanted to because some kid tripped Lucy."

"I tripped him back," Lucy adds. "So Sophie wouldn't hit him."

"What kind of soccer league do they play in?" Morgan laughs. I turn the phone to show her sitting on the bed.

"Morgan?"

"Morgan!"

"Where's Carson? Did she come with you?"

"How come she got to come when we couldn't?" Sophie demands.

"Because she's a baby and we're not," Ben explains to his sister.

"Did you hear we're having a baby?" Lucy cries.

What?

"What?" My shock echoes in Morgan's expression.

"No one is having a baby. The only thing happening now is that you three need to go to bed," I say weakly.

"Wait, I didn't get to say goodnight," Lucy shrieks.

Three rounds of goodnights and *I love yous* to me, a round of good nights to Morgan and many blown kisses later, J.B. finally takes back the phone.

"I didn't tell her to say that," he says quietly.

"I'll deal with you *later*," I threaten. "Good luck getting them to sleep."

"Have fun whatever you do tonight," he says. "Morgan, keep her out of trouble."

"We're hitting the town tonight," Morgan promises. "But first, we're going to have a little chat about this baby thing."

"It's not a thing," I mutter. I say goodnight to J.B., and blow him kisses, as affectionate as the kids were. As soon as I end the call, Morgan is staring at me with accusing eyes.

"Are you pregnant?" she hisses.

"No."

"But Lucy says–"

"Lucy wants a baby. Apparently, all the kids do." I take a deep breath. "And so does J.B.," I announce dramatically, with a glance over my shoulder at the door to make sure Brit isn't within hearing distance.

Morgan leans forward. "When did this happen?"

"The day after Brit told us about this trip, so I've had a bit on my mind. I was going to tell you–"

"When we got home," she finishes. "But J.B. wants one? *Him*, not you?"

"Yes, *him*. I've never even thought about it. Maybe I've thought it, but I've never said it," I confess.

Morgan's eyes light up with excitement. "Are you going to have another? Because then Carson will be the big girl to someone!"

This makes me instantly regret telling her. I want someone to tell me I'm crazy, not get me excited enough to toss out the birth control pills when I get home. "I don't know."

"It's a no-brainer. You love kids, Casey, and if J.B. wants more too–"

"I don't know. I'm used to three, but four seems a lot. And what if–?" I flop face-first on the bed.

"You have triplets again?" Morgan finishes for me.

"Exactly," I say as I roll to my side. "It's something I really have to think about because it's a pretty good possibility that I'll have more than one. I can't say anything to Brit about it because she'll have a fit and say my kids are ruining her weekend."

"Then we better keep quiet because the water has stopped." She beams at me. "Another baby."

"You really think it's a good idea? You don't think I'm too old?"

"You're not even forty-two. Gwen Stefani was older than that. And so was Halle Berry and...You're not thinking of that book again, are you?"

A Young Woman's Guide to Impending Pregnancy had been my bible since my mother passed it to me in my twenties. It has a lot of great tips and advice, despite being written in 1942 by a quack of a doctor who believed women over thirty-seven should not conceive. It caused a great deal of stress when I turned thirty-five, but some could say it was the catalyst to me getting pregnant. It sounds better than saying a drunken night and an expired condom got me pregnant.

I don't have time to answer Morgan before Brit bursts out of the bathroom, clad only in a towel and frowns when she sees Morgan and me still on the bed where she left us. "Aren't you ready?" she cries.

"You're not," I point out.

"Five minutes," she promises.

To give Brit credit, nine minutes later the three of us are standing on the terrace with glasses in our hands watching the Bellagio fountain rise and fall in a rainbow of colours. The setting sun is a beacon for the lights of The Strip to come alive.

"I've never seen anything like this," I marvel.

"Glad you came?"

I glance over, the setting sun softening Brit's face. She worked wonders in those nine minutes, reapplying her makeup, and a quick fix of her hair. Her red pencil skirt and sleeveless blouse are a little formal for me but does a great job highlighting her figure. No extra baby weight there.

"I wouldn't miss it for the world." I push away any thoughts of my earlier reluctance. J.B. was right once again. I need to be here.

"I wouldn't have done it without you," Brit admits in a low voice. "It would have seemed wrong if you weren't able to come."

Touched, I lean my head on her shoulder, vowing to give my oldest friend my full attention. The kids are fine tucked in back home with J.B. This is my time–mine and Brit's–to celebrate her happiness.

"To us," Morgan says loudly, holding up her glass. "To having fun and leaving responsibilities at home."

It's like she can read my mind. Morgan's good like that.

"To us," I second, clinking my glass against hers.

***

Our first stop in Brit's Weekend to Remember–my name for it, not hers–is the first of many bars in the hotel. It's called The Study with a casual, library vibe which I love, but Brit dismisses. We have a glass of champagne and the waitress tells us about the other bars in the hotel.

"You really don't have to leave the hotel," she says. "There's so much to do here."

Next stop is dinner at *Estiatorio Milo*.

"This is nice," I say as I glance critically at the tables. "Good space, but *Thrice* has a better atmosphere; a few of the mains dishes can compare to what Cooper can do at *Thrice*, but the wine list here is amazing." I make a mental note to help J.B. with that.

When I work at the restaurant, it's as an unofficial sommelier. Before the kids came along, I used to supplement my teaching salary by working in a wine store, so even bartender J.B. admits that I know my stuff.

Brit scoffs at my blasé comment. "You're seriously comparing this place to Cooper's restaurant? This is a world-class place in Las Vegas."

"And *Thrice* is number six of Toronto's top restaurants; Toronto is also a world-class city, in case you haven't noticed. I think Cooper would do well for himself here."

"I can totally see J.B. behind the bar at that *Vesper* bar the waitress told us about," Morgan cuts in.

"He'd love the James Bond vibe," I agree. "He's teaching the kids how to make martinis. Says it's a life skill. Lucy says–"

Brit sets her Lychee martini on the table a little harder than necessary. Once again, she's matched her drink to her nail polish. "We're not talking about the kids tonight. Or tomorrow. Or the next night. This weekend is for the over-eighteen crowds only."

Before I can comment with words I most likely will regret, Brit continues, turning to me with a vulnerable expression that I don't normally see. "I want this weekend to be like when we were younger. After we graduated when we didn't have responsibilities. When we could do whatever we wanted and didn't have to explain ourselves. Before boyfriends, or husbands, or *kids*. When it was just the three of us." Brit turns to include Morgan and then back to me. "Who knows when we can do this again? I want it to be just *us* this weekend, just like it used to be."

I meet Morgan's gaze, both of us surprised at Brit's pleading tone. "I don't remember a time before boyfriends," Morgan says. "You two never had anyone serious, but I had Anil for years–"

"I can't believe you let him come to your wedding after they broke up," I accuse Brit.

"I can't believe how you ruined my wedding by getting into a fight with his new girlfriend," Brit shot back at Morgan.

"She started it." Morgan grins. "But I definitely finished it."

The moment passes and we start talking about Brit's weddings–never her marriages, but the memorable parts of her wedding days. Like during her second wedding, when her sister Sierra smoke a little too much weed before the ceremony. It was like a remake of the wedding scene from *Sixteen Candles*, where the sister takes the muscle relaxant and chats to the guests on the way down the aisle. Sierra did more than chat; she touched, she hugged, she grabbed the crotch of one of Brick's friends.

Brit's third wedding was smaller, with only Morgan and I as attendants.

"I haven't heard much of your wedding plans," Morgan says as we're served our first courses. "What more do you have to do?"

Brit picks up one of her oysters and slurps it down before answering. "Not a lot. I've been focused on this weekend."

"What's Justin doing for his bachelor party?" I ask, taking a fork to my shrimp but eyeing Brit's plate. I forgot how much I love Rockefeller oysters.

"We're not talking about Justin because if we talk about him, you'll start talking about J.B., and that will lead back to the kids," Brit says with an edge to her voice. *"Just us."*

I fight the urge to roll my eyes. "I'll make sure I don't mention him if you give me one of your oysters."

"Get your own oysters." Brit slurps down a second one.

"Trade you for two of my shrimp," I offer.

"Deal."

CHAPTER THIRTEEN

All relationships formed after the child is born should somehow benefit the baby.

A Young Woman's Guide to Raising Obedient Children
Dr. Francine Pascal Reid, (1943)

I stick to my promise to give Brit a weekend to remember and keep the conversation off of men or kids with difficulty.

After dinner, we stop for dry martinis at *Vesper*.

"J.B would love this place," I muse as we're shown to our seats. But that's all I say about him.

We move on to the funky *Bond*, where a creepy guy does his best to pick us up. Offensive, but it's been a long time since anyone tried to pick me up so I'm a little flattered.

I mentally make note of the cocktails in the *CliQue* bar to pass on to J.B. The drinks are delicious and potent and give me the courage to suggest we try the nightclub to dance. But the liquid courage doesn't last long when it's apparent that we are the oldest ones in the place. Brit's inability to get served at the bar sends us running to the Chandelier nightclub.

And at two-thirty in the morning, we're still here, watching Brit do shots with another bride-to-be, who must be about half her age.

"Why are we the only ones here?" I try my best to hide the yawn that splits my face, but Morgan sees it and smiles.

"Is Casey tired?" she mocks in a singsong voice.

"Casey is sleeping with her eyes open. Can't you tell?" I glance over my shoulder at Brit, talking and laughing and still going strong despite steadily drinking all night. I switched to water hours ago. "I want to bail but I can't leave her here."

Gone are the days when I could party all night. These days, staying up past ten-thirty is an accomplishment.

Morgan gives me a sympathetic smile. "Why don't you head back to the room? I'll drag her back when she starts to run out of steam." We both glance at Brit again, who is laughing uproariously at something the bartender has said. "She has to run out of steam soon, doesn't she?"

I make no effort to hide my sigh of frustration. "When she divorced Brick, we closed down that bar, remember?"

"But she was sad then. She's happy that she's getting married, isn't she?"

"I think so. But you'd think after the last time...Serves her right for marrying a guy named Brick." Brick had been Brit's second husband, close after Tom divorced her after only a few months. Brit had an affair with Tom's boss, who refused to leave his wife and left Brit in the lurch. Brick helped console her; that marriage lasted two years before Brick moved on to console someone else.

"Was that really his name?" Morgan wonders. "Or a nickname?"

UNEXPECTINGLY HAPPILY EVER AFTER

"Brit and Brick." I shake my head. "That should have been a red flag right there."

I swear, sometimes her life is worse than a soap opera."

Morgan nudges me. "Check out what just walked in the door. Can we have him in the soap opera?"

I glance over and my jaw literally drops. "Fuck a duck—what's *that?*"

A group of men walks in, wearing nothing fancier than baggy jeans and white T-shirts but commanding the attention of every woman in the place by the way they wear those jeans and simple shirts. I've never seen better bodies.

J.B. still looks good, but my hubby has nothing on these boys.

It's as if a scene from *Magic Mike* has come to life. Even though these boys still have their clothes on, even though my experience with male dancers has been once when I was twenty, and once when I was thirty-four, I can tell in an instant that these guys are strippers.

"Close your mouth, Casey!" Morgan laughs. "I think they're coming over."

The group of seven extremely sexy men do come our way but bypass us for Brit's little bride-to-be friend and her group. They saunter, they swagger, they exude arrogance with every step. Normally, I'm turned off by such a display of raw cockiness, but I'm tired and they're very good-looking.

And in a matter of minutes, they succeed in returning Brit to us.

"Asshats," she grumbles after weaving her way through the throng of bodies. It was as if every available person in the place flocks to the dancers, males as well as females.

"Are you too old for them?" I ask her sympathetically. Brit is all about fighting off each and every sign of aging and as a result, she can easily pass for thirty-three rather than forty-three. She looks good, even at ten-thirty in the morning.

But her little bride friend is twenty-five if she's a day, and cute as a button. And her three bridesmaids all have impressive chest measurements that haven't been impacted by the sands of time. As good as Brit looks, there's no competing with that.

"They're looking to get laid," Brit says dismissively. "And I'm not."

"Who are they?" Morgan asks. I can't help but notice her attention has been caught by one of the men. All of them must be at least six-five; they tower over the group like the women are children.

"Tower of Power, Power Tower–something like that. They're strippers, Morgan, can't you tell? A cheap version of *Thunder from Down Under*."

"They don't seem cheap to me," I muse. I notice Morgan has caught the eye of one of them–taller than the others, bald, and with a chest as broad as the Mississippi. He gives her a shy smile. His smile triggers a memory. "Hang on a sec." I fish in my back pocket and pull out the flyer which has molded nicely to my backside. "A guy gave me this in the casino. I think it was him."

We stare at the paper advertising *The Power of the Tower*. And from the looks of it, Morgan's new admirer is at the centre of whatever power we're talking about.

"He's a stripper?" Morgan whispers, her face falling.

"So?" Without giving her a chance to stop me, I stalk toward Shy Smile. To give him credit, he moves away from the group when he sees me coming.

"What is she doing?" I hear Brit after me.

"Was that you in the casino earlier?" I wave the flyer at him.

"Ah, the lady of the coins," he says, his smile widening. He's very cute, with dimples and everything. I glance back to see Morgan, eyes wide and staring.

"I still haven't cashed them in," I say. "I had to pick up my friends. That's them over there." I gesture to where Morgan is now shaking her head frantically. "That's Brit, who's getting married, and Morgan, who's not."

"Not getting married, or isn't married?" he wonders.

"Not married at all." I grin. "Would you like to meet her?"

And it's as easy as that. I usher Brit off to the side after a few minutes because it seems like Morgan is doing just fine.

I like the way she smiles at him. I'm not sure how a man larger than The Rock, aka Dwayne Johnson, can look sweet, but this guy does. Sweet and shy and–

"*What* is she doing?" Brit hisses as we watch them.

"*She's* talking to him, so let's give her a minute." Brit huffs a response and taps her foot with annoyance. "Give her a minute," I repeat. "She hasn't met anyone in a while."

"Being a single mother will do that to you."

"Now who's talking about kids?"

"She can talk to him for however long she wants, but he's a stripper, Casey, and this is Las Vegas. What does she expect to get out of this?"

I cock my head and stare at Brit. "What do you think she wants out of this?"

Brit flips her hair. I suspect most of her annoyance comes from the utter lack of attention she received from the men. "Not in my room."

"I wouldn't mind a bed to myself tonight," I muse.

Morgan only makes us wait about ten minutes. "Don't wait for me," she says, touching my shoulder with a starry-eyed smile. "Go on to the room. We're going to get coffee."

I haven't seen that smile on her face in a long time. Nerves and excitement and *whatamIdoing* and *I thinkImightlikehim* all rolled into one toothy grin.

"Coffee, huh?" I narrow my eyes at the brute standing behind her. Either this guy is a good enough player to fool Morgan, or he really is a nice guy. And it's not easy to fool Morgan. The girl is *smart*, plus ever since she opened her own PR firm a few years ago, she's developed the best built-in asshole detector. Because of this, I'm not as worried about leaving her as I would be about Brit.

Plus, not that Morgan would ever say anything, but I think she's desperate to pick up. She hasn't been in a relationship since she broke up with Derek–my step-uncle– long story–two years ago. I know one of the reasons she agreed to this weekend was the slim possibility of getting laid.

"I'll have her back to your room in an hour." His voice growls like a dump truck and I have to crane my neck to look up at him. The lights of the chandelier gleam off his bald head. Is that an accent I hear amid the noise of the bar?

"Well, that's no fun," Brit says *sotto voce*.

"He's Canadian too," Morgan says proudly. "From Newfoundland. We're neighbours."

Morgan's family is from Nova Scotia, so *neighbours* is a bit of a stretch.

"If you're sure," I pretend to relent, narrowing my eyes at the Newfie.

"I'm sure," Morgan says with an even wider smile. "Really, Casey."

"She's fine, let's get out of here." Brit grabs my arm, frog-marching me out of the bar. I'm relieved to be heading back to the room, but Morgan...

A last look behind shows that Morgan will be just fine.

Chapter Fourteen

> Friendships should be cherished with other women; know that other non-mothers might feel resentment and bitterness for the amount of time you spend on your children.
>
> *A Young Woman's Guide to Raising Obedient Children*
> Dr. Francine Pascal Reid, (1943)

"His name is *Bron?*" Brit screeches the next morning. "His name's actually *Ron* but because of his size, they always called him brawny Ronnie. So now he's Bron." Despite the late night, Morgan is the first one awake, showered, and ready.

"Just how big is he?" Brit asks, still in her satin pajamas. She's not asking Morgan how tall Bron is.

"We had coffee last night. Only coffee," Morgan assures us. I still had to share the bed with her last night; I had been both impressed and slightly disappointed that she returned to the hotel room moments before the promised one hour. "He's taking me to breakfast this morning."

"Are you sure he's a stripper?" Brit asks despairingly. "I thought they were all drinking and drugs and sex after shows."

"He's nice," Morgan protests. "He's not like that."

I glance at Morgan. I've known her for almost twenty-five years, and while Morgan tends to keep her feelings tucked close to her chest, unlike more emotional me, I've learned to read her long ago.

She likes this guy. She likes him a lot.

"You've been watching too much *Magic Mike*," I say to Brit. "I'm sure they're not all like that."

"He's getting us tickets for the show tonight," Morgan promises. "The Power of the Tower. It's always sold out."

"That's nice of him. I guess he wants you to see him dance."

"Actually, he doesn't," Morgan laughs. "He says he'll be too self-conscious with me in the audience. But I begged him. I said if I was going to be getting to know him better, I need to see it for myself, rather than imagining the worst."

"You're going to be getting to know him better?" I ask at the same time Brit cries out. "Strippers are not self-conscious! Who is this guy?"

Morgan only shrugs with a soft expression in her eyes. "He's Bron."

"At least you're getting something out of it. We have appointments at the spa in an hour," Brit reminds her.

"I might be a little late for that," Morgan hedges, heading for the door.

And then she's gone, not giving me a chance to ask what the heck was going on.

"I can't believe she just did that," Brit says in a quiet voice after the door closes behind her.

"She must really like him."

"Well, she needs to like me better since I organized this weekend to celebrate our friendship," Brit says in a haughty voice.

"Celebrate our friendship?" I echo. "That's nice enough, but I thought this was your stagette?"

Brit gives a wave. "That's what all the little girls from last night called it. Hens' nights. Bachelorette parties. I'm beyond that."

She stalks through the room, heading for the terrace. Her focus seems to be shifted away from Morgan, but I can read Brit even better than Morgan and something is off. "Have you talked to Justin?" I ask as she pulls open the door. We're high enough that the sounds from The Strip are a faint buzz, like white noise.

"This is a *girls'* weekend, so why would I talk to him?"

"I'm going to talk to J.B. now," I call as she steps outside.

"If you must."

It's not like I need her permission. I connect to FaceTime. Even though I'm sleep rumpled and still wearing last night's makeup, the good thing about being married is that J.B. has undoubtedly seen me look worse.

With the time difference, it pains me that I've missed seeing the kids before they went to school, but J.B.'s smiling face answers the call. "Hey, babe."

"Are the kids okay?"

"And I miss you too. Are you having fun? The kids are fine–sent them off to school with money for lunch."

"You have to send them food for lunch!" That's the grin I love, the one that shows his dimple. "I miss them."

"I know. They miss you too." He runs a hand through his hair, mussing it up. It's eleven-thirty back in Toronto and usually, he would be getting ready to head to the restaurant. But I can tell he's wearing one of those soft T-shirts that stretch at his broad shoulders, so he must be working from home. I can't believe how good it is to see J.B. It's only been twenty-four hours but all I want to do is stare at the phone, rememorizing the lines and curves of his face. I wish I was home so I could throw my arms around him and press my nose into his chest to breathe in his J.B. smell.

But if I wasn't here, I would be at school, with eighteen 5-year-olds, breathing in their special scent of glue and crayons.

"Tell me what trouble you've gotten into," J.B. demands with another grin, this one that has the butterflies in my stomach taking flight, even after six years of marriage.

"Morgan met a man," I report. "He's a stripper."

"Do I want to know how she met him?"

"Perfectly innocently—we were at a bar and he had all his clothes on. But she's got us tickets to see his show tonight."

J.B. raises an eyebrow. "That will be interesting."

"Do you mind? Because I'm not asking permission."

"You shouldn't have to." He frowns. "Do you want me to mind?"

"Not really. What's been going on there?" I ask eagerly. "Kids, you..."

"Nothing exciting since we talked to you last night. They loved the video from the casino, by the way. How much did you win?"

"I still haven't gone back to cash it in," I admit, making a mental note to do that today. I tell him about last night, what we ate in the restaurant and because he's into mixology, the different bars, and clubs, and drinks we had.

I glance up when Brit comes in from the terrace.

"Are you still talking?"

UNEXPECTINGLY HAPPILY EVER AFTER

I wave the phone at her. "Hi Brit," J.B says, pasting a smile on his face. He does his best, but Brit's never been his favourite person. He gets along much better with Morgan. "Happy bachelorette party."

"Hi, J.B. Do you want to get breakfast when you're done talking?"

"I would love to go to breakfast with you, Brit," J.B. replies.

"Unfortunately, you're not invited," Brit says rudely. "Casey? I'm famished."

Famished means she might have an egg with her yogurt and fruit. "Yep, I'm hungry. Just a sec." I turn back to J.B.'s face. "I'll try and call when the kids are home from school."

"If you can't, don't worry. Your sister invited us for dinner tonight. Apparently, she doesn't think I'm capable of feeding my children. Wonder how she got that idea?"

"I didn't say anything about cooking," I protest. "I miss you."

"I miss you too. Stay out of trouble."

"No promises." I kiss the screen and end the call. When I look up, Brit is staring at me.

"You're still so sappy."

For once, her comment doesn't sound like a criticism. I shrug. "I still love him."

"Well, I don't expect that will change but you're always so *miss you, love you, mwah, mwah, mwah.*" She makes kissing faces to go with the sound effects.

"I'm sorry if it offends you," I say stiffly.

"It doesn't offend me." She pauses and I pull myself off the bed, thinking that she's finished. But she's not. "It–you're the only one of the three of us to have found that with someone. I guess I've never realized how rare that is, that kind of love."

Mystified, I only stare at her. Was that a compliment about my relationship? But before I can ask, her expression tightens. "Get dressed. Let's go get something to eat."

I get dressed in record time and Brit and I find a suitable place for breakfast. As much as I try to bring the conversation back around, it's clear Brit is back on her no- talking-about-men mantra.

I watch her eat blueberry pancakes swimming in syrup. It's a first for her. In all the years we've been friends, I've never witnessed Brit enjoying a meal when we go out. She goes for the low-fat, no-flavour things when we're out in public.

It's not just this morning; last night she had pasta for dinner, plus dessert. Her own–no sharing like I sometimes do with Morgan.

"Why are you staring at me?" Brit interrupts my observation.

"Because I never see you eat like this," I tell her honestly.

Brit shrugs as she forks up another mouthful of pancakes. I went for the eggs Benedict like I always do, but for once am regretting my decision. The pancakes look good.

"Is everything okay?"

She meets my gaze with a steely-eyed look. "Why do you ask?"

"Because...you're eating. And you seem more anti-men than usual. I can't put my finger on it."

Brit gives me a roll of her eye. "I'm not anti-men."

"Anti-our men, then. More than usual. Normally you would have gotten all the details out of Morgan about last night by now."

"I don't think there were many details to be had. They had coffee."

There's a hint of irritation in her voice, more than usual. "You're being a bitch," I say in a quiet voice. "More than usual."

Brit stares at her plate. "I know."

Brit has always been a difficult person to like, with her lack of empathy for my issues and hard-ass approach to life. But she's very easy to love when she lets down her guard, which she's done many times in our years of friendship. And she's always been there for me when I needed her the most, just like I always have been for her.

"Could you stop?" I ask. No accusation. There's no need. Brit is almost as close to me as my sister, which is why she treats me like she does.

And I don't bother asking her what's bothering her. I know Brit will tell me when she's ready.

"I'll try."

I nod and return to my eggs. "What's Lacey up to these days?"

I can tell Brit is making an effort to sound less bitchy as she tells me the latest hijinks her younger sister Lacey has gotten up to. The cloud seems to pass from her face as we talk and begin to laugh together, and by the end of the meal, I'm once again reminded that Brit can be fun.

It's nice to have a day with her.

We don't see Morgan until the middle of the afternoon when she finds us sunning by the pool. Her hands are full of daiquiris. "I brought gifts," she says with a nervous glance at Brit. Morgan missed the morning at the spa, the hours Brit and I spent wandering the shops of the hotel. Both of us would have liked to explore The Strip, but there was so much to see right there in the hotel.

I brace myself for the tongue-lashing guilt trip, prepared to jump in to save Morgan.

"You better bring more than gifts," Brit says, reaching for one of the daiquiris. "We expect details."

Chapter Fifteen

Excess excitement should be avoided at all costs for new mothers.

A Young Woman's Guide to Raising Obedient Children
Dr. Francine Pascal Reid, (1943)

"I can't believe he gave you tickets for this," I squeal, practically bouncing on my seat from excitement.

After lounging by the pool, we changed for dinner, peppering Morgan with questions about Bron—what he was like, what happened, what she wanted to happen. Morgan has a history of falling hard and fast for men, but I've never seen her so smitten.

"Did you tell him about Carson?" Brit asked, during our first course at dinner. Once again she got something normal people would eat and enjoy, without a word about how much weight she would undoubtedly gain during this trip.

"I told him about Carson, Derek, Anil–everything." Morgan's eyes were bright, the smile permanently etched onto her face. "He told me about his marriage, his kids, whom he hardly ever sees. They live in Moncton."

"And he's here," I said with sympathy.

"He doesn't want to do this forever," Morgan had explained. "He's thirty-eight, and he's only got a few more years before he's too old. But he's tired of this life."

My excitement for the show only builds during dinner, but Morgan gets quieter as the evening goes on. And now we're crammed into our seats, shoulder to shoulder with hundreds of screaming, panting women, begging for the show to begin, and Morgan has a concerned expression on her face.

I lean closer to her. "You don't look happy to be here."

Morgan glances warily at the stage. Music blares, lights flash, heightening the excitement of the audience. "I don't know if I want to see that side of him," she admits in a quiet voice.

"You really like him?"

Morgan shrugs with a helpless smile. "He's *so* sweet, nothing like you'd imagine a dancer would be like."

"Stripper."

"*Dancer*," she corrects with a frown. "He says he keeps his underwear on."

"I don't know what you call that, but I don't think it's underwear," I point out as the first dancer appears on stage.

It doesn't take long for Morgan to get caught up in the excitement. There's not a lot not to like watching men with beautiful bodies writhe on stage.

The best part is watching the other women in the audience. Some of them barely retain control of themselves, screaming and yelling and begging the men to do all sorts of nasty things to them. I notice Morgan wincing at some of the more lurid comments as she waits for Bron to make his entrance.

I clap as the dancers leave the stage, the waistbands of their g-strings full of bills. "These guys must make a fortune!" I say to Morgan.

"Bron says it's pretty lucrative but it's not something he wants to do for much longer. He says—"

But whatever Morgan is about to say is drowned out by the booming voice over the loudspeaker. "Aaannd now…our *veeerry* own Tower of Power—the beast himself!"

Lights flash frantically before the stage darkens except for a spotlight. And Bron appears.

"Holy shit, Morgan!" Brit screams, clapping her hands like a little girl. "You got a piece of that last night?"

"It wasn't like that. And it was this morning. After breakfast." Even with the flashing strobe lights, I notice Morgan's cheeks are pink.

Bron's size is impressive but his dance skills are truly amazing. I've never seen a man his height dance like that. He pops, he thrusts, he twerks. I don't know the name of most of what he does, nor do I care. I stand watching him dance with my mouth open, my only thought *Morgan had* him?

Partway through Bron's performance, I suddenly turn to Morgan and give her a high five. She laughs self-consciously, her fingers twining with mine to give my hand a squeeze.

She likes him. She met the man not even twenty-four hours ago, and she already likes him.

Out of the corner of my eye, I see a heavyset woman launch herself onto the stage. She doesn't exactly make it all the way, and she's left with her torso lying flat a few feet away from a gyrating Bron, her legs dangling in the faces of those on their feet yelling for more.

One of her black flats flies off her foot, right into my face. I rear back in shock.

"Are you okay?" Morgan demands.

"I think so." I pick up the shoe–a leather ballet flat, size nine. Too big for me. I hurl it back into the crowd, hitting a woman on the back of the head and ducking behind Morgan when the woman turns around.

But our attention is quickly caught again by the action on the stage. While Bron continues to dance, a second woman makes her own attempt to get on the stage, using the first women's prone body, to clamber up.

There's cheering and shouts of encouragement as she heaves herself on top of the first woman, who wriggles and struggles to push her off as she continues to clamber onto the stage. Her shirt is pushed up, with love handles that have seen no love lately are displayed.

I can't look away.

The second woman is finally tipped off, and the two of them lay there, torsos on the stage, legs dangling and without the upper body strength to pull themselves up.

"Where is security?" Morgan cries. "Why don't they stop them?"

"They look like two beached whales," Brit laughs. "There's no stopping that."

I laugh, hating to admit that Brit is right. Pale flesh that hasn't seen the sun nor a gym in a long time is revealed as they struggle to be the first to ascent their own private Everest.

Bron dances closer, his presence urging the women on.

"Stop them!" Morgan shouts.

"There's no stopping them," I tell her, Brit clutching my arm as we laugh.

But then Morgan darts in front of me, heading for the stage. "Morgan, don't!"

But Morgan does.

Morgan is strong and tough and fighting for her man. And she has a temper. During Brit's first wedding, she caused a scene by knocking out her ex's new girlfriend with one punch. In Morgan's defense, the new girlfriend was throwing wine glasses, one of them hitting me. It was only after I got hit that she decked the girl. She's very protective of those she loves.

I watch in horror/admiration as Morgan grabs the second woman by the waist and yanks her off the stage. As she grabs the legs of the first woman, she's surrounded by a mob of angry women before she can manhandle the woman off of the stage. I catch sight of Morgan's blond hair once before she vanishes.

"Morgan!" Brit shouts.

I look at Brit, and Brit looks at me and without a word, we both jump into the melee caused by Morgan defending her new man.

Chapter Sixteen

Women need time to bond and should look for any opportunity to do so. It will only benefit the child to have a mother with a firm support system.

A Young Woman's Guide to Raising Obedient Children
Dr. Francine Pascal Reid, (1943)

We are told later that women climbing onstage were a usual occurrence at one of the *Power of the Tower* shows. Bron was the tallest tower, and therefore the focus of the women's efforts.

No one had ever tried to stop them. It was like a rite of passage to get on stage, and only a few have ever succeeded. Security only concerns themselves if someone gets up, and when that happens, Bron gives them a hug and a kiss and sends them on their way. No one took kindly to Morgan's endeavors to protect Bron from the crowd of lovesick women. And many saw her as a threat to their quest. A bit of pushing and pulling soon collapses into a seething, sprawling girl fight that took over the first five rows of the audience.

Security can't contain the fight as it grows and the police are called.

What is ironic is that Morgan gets away scot-free, while Brit and I, as well as a dozen other women, are arrested.

Which is how I find myself in jail for the first time in my life.

***

"This is all Morgan's fault!"

It's the sixth time Brit has announced that. It's getting more difficult to defend Morgan from behind bars, trapped in a holding cell with at least fifteen women. The smell is horrific–a mixture of sweat, rancid body odor, too much perfume, and alcohol fumes.

I hear the retching and turn away just in time. Can't forget the smell of vomit.

"I've never even been in a police station before," Brit mutters, grasping the bars like it's a lifeline.

"First time for everything."

Keeping positive is becoming as much of a chore as defending Morgan, but if I don't, I'll end up in a sodden heap of tears, badmouthing everyone and everything with Brit. At least I've sobered up.

The singing from the back corner begins again reminding me that not everyone has.

"I hope the kids are okay."

"Well, they're not in jail with us, so I don't know why they wouldn't be," Brit says, picking at her nails.

Instinctively, I cover her hand with mine to stop it. "Stop picking."

"I'm not."

"You pick when you're nervous."

"I'm not nervous!"

I glance at her, scrutinizing her expression. Even if I hadn't known her most of my life, I could still tell something was wrong. "Morgan will get us out," I soothe. "We won't be in here for long."

"I'll never be able to get the smell out of my clothes. I'll have to burn them."

"I think that's a bit drastic."

Brit turns to me, blue eyes furious. "Do you not understand what's going on here, Casey? We're in *jail*. We've been arrested for *fighting*. At a *strip club*. How can you not think this is the most horrible night of your life?"

"Plus you hit like a girl," a woman in the throng behind us says.

Brit whirls around. "That's because I am a *girl!* I'm a woman and unlike some of you *heathens,* I'm not accustomed to using my fists to solve my issues. And why the hell would anyone want to climb up on the stage? Did you think those guys were going to pull you up, forget about the hundreds of dollars in their g-strings and whisk you away? No! Those men would take your money and push you away, just like every other man in the world!"

"Brit," I murmur, my hand on her arm. It's not the first outburst of the evening. There's been a variety of cursing, crying, shouting, and downright hysterics since we've been locked up.

It's been forty-seven minutes since we've been incarcerated. Apparently, that's the limit for Brit.

"Morgan will get us out," I repeat, trying to sound like I know Morgan's whereabouts. I don't. The sight of her blond head as the women leaped on her was the last I saw of her. I left her a message on her cell, but I have no idea if she got it. I hope she's okay.

"How do you know? She's probably off screwing that Power Tower and forgot all about us," Brit sneers.

There's a rumble behind us. It's impossible to have a private conversation here. "She better not touch Bron."

"He's mine."

"I gave him fifty bucks, and I'm damn well going home with that boy tonight."

I cringe and try to forget what I've heard. "Morgan won't forget us."

"I lost my cousin too," a blond says from the bench against the wall. "They couldn't have gotten everyone. It wasn't even that bad of a fight."

Brit whirls around but stops herself when she catches sight of the white dress the woman is wearing. "You look like you should be at a wedding."

"I was. But it got canceled."

I close my eyes, waiting for the next bout of bad temper, but Brit surprises me by leaning against the bars to face the blond. "So what happened?" Brit demands. "He dump you?"

"*She* walked out on *him*," the friend says proudly. She lifts a hand for a high five, which the blond reluctantly slaps. "So proud of you."

The blond sighs. "I don't know what happened. One minute I was walking down the aisle and Thomas turned and smiled at me, and I knew I couldn't marry him." She glances at the dark-haired woman leaning against her shoulder. "You never thought I should marry him."

The brunette presses her lips together in a firm line. "I'm pleading the fifth at least until you talk to him."

"So you had no reason for dumping him? Just like that—it's over?" I wince at the venom in Brit's voice. "That's pretty shitty."

The blond's face falls. "Brit!" I admonish.

"Flora has her reasons," the friend announces in an icy voice. "And they're none of your business."

Flora waves her hand. "It's okay, M.K. And it was a pretty shitty thing to do."

Brit harrumphs and turns away, once more gripping the bars. "I'm sure you have your reasons," I say. "I apologize for my friend. She's a bit upset. This is her stagette and it got a bit messed up."

Brit whirls around. "This is *not* my stagette! Will you stop telling people that?"

"It's my stagette too," says a girl with a ripped *Bride-to-be* sash around her shoulders.

"Mine too," echoes another.

"Well, it's not mine." Brit's mutter is so low that only I hear her.

"What are you talking about?" I demand. "This is what we're here for because you're getting married! I left my kids to spend the weekend with you because you're getting married. I used my one phone call to call Morgan. Did you even call Justin and tell him what's going on?"

Brit refuses to meet my eyes. "It's not like he can do anything to help."

"But he might—you've hardly mentioned him." The realization hits me like the shoe clocking me on the side of the head had earlier. "What's going on?"

"Unlike you, Casey, I keep my thoughts to myself."

"No, you don't. You're getting married in a few weeks. Justin should be all you're talking about." I stand, hands on hips, demanding answers.

Brit turns her head away from me.

"What happened? Did you get in a fight?"

Brit snorts, such an odd sound coming from her. "About five weeks ago."

"What happened?" I repeat. "Did he not like you coming here? What's his problem?"

"His problem, apparently, is me. We broke up." Her tone is casual like she's reciting a menu.

"What?" My tone is anything but. "What are you talking about? When? Why? Why didn't you tell me? Brit, what's going on?" Brit shrugs, looking more vulnerable then she has in years. I move closer and touch her arm. "What happened?"

She sighs heavily. "It's over. He met someone else–someone he liked better. I guess he met her around the same time as he met me, dated both of us, picked me and then changed his mind when the wedding plans were made. He got in touch with her; she still had feelings…" she trails off with another shrug.

"Sounds like the last season of *The Bachelor*." My mind swirls with questions and I'm sure I'm gaping like a fish, but I don't know what to say. Comfort? Get angry on her behalf? Sympathy? Jokey comments?

And deep down, in that low place, I don't want to acknowledge, I can't help but think Brit might have deserved it.

"Let me get this straight," I begin. "You're not getting married?"

"Not anytime soon," Brit says bitterly.

"But–"

"You think I deserve it."

"Of course I don't," I lie.

"You think because I'm such a bitch–You even told me I was being a bitch earlier, so why wouldn't Justin think that? Why wouldn't he pick someone nicer?"

"I'm not thinking that. I don't know what I'm thinking. Are you okay?" Brit only shrugs. "Why didn't you tell me?" I keep my voice quiet, even though I want to scream it at her. Brit is my best friend, so why on earth wouldn't she tell me?

We came to Las Vegas because she was getting married again.

She gives me a tight-lipped smile. "It's not the easiest thing to admit to. It's embarrassing."

"Seriously?" I reel back, holding tight to my temper. Now is not the time to be upset that she's dragged me away from my children. "Brit, you've seen me with my head stuck in a toilet. I've helped you pee when you were wearing your wedding dress. This is nothing to be embarrassed about. I would have hated him for you. I would have stalked the other girl on social media."

Brit doesn't say anything for a long moment, staring out the bars and refusing to meet my eyes. I ignore the crying and conversation behind us, praying no one will interrupt.

"It's been...hard. I've watched you and J.B. Before him, you were a mess. I had the better relationships, the hotter guys, but then you got pregnant and got married."

"It's not a competition!"

"It is for me," she confesses. "It always has been. That's just who I am. Not a great trait, I know."

"You think?"

"We're not criticizing my character traits—"

"I'm not exactly sure what we're doing! You drop this bombshell on me, tell me you've been jealous of me, the wedding is off. Forgive me for being a bit confused."

"I never said I was jealous. But you have everything you've always wanted, Casey. As happy as I am for you, I can't help feeling sad for myself."

I pause. Whatever I think of Brit, I've only wanted happiness for her. We planned our lives out—She was going to have a grand, sweeping epic life, and I was going to have a more comfortable, but still amazing future. We were both going to find our happily ever afters.

But only one of us did.

"So what are you going to do?" I ask after a long pause, broken by more retching in the corner.

"What can I do? It's over with Justin. We're not getting married."

"But you brought us all the way to Las Vegas for a bachelorette party!" I burst out.

Brit smiles sadly. "I've always wanted to go to Vegas with you, Casey. I thought this was as good a time as any. I keep waiting for you to announce you're pregnant again."

I keep my mouth shut. Now is not the time for true confessions from me.

"I know you didn't want to come," she adds sadly.

"It not that I didn't want to come, but I have three kids, Brit. It's really hard for me to get away. J.B. can handle them but they're my responsibility. You don't understand." I bite my tongue as soon as the words leave my mouth. I've always tiptoed around the topic of the kids with Brit, just like we've always skirted the subject of why she doesn't want kids.

"No, I clearly don't." Brit's tone is as icy as the prison floor. "But do you ever stop to think that *I'm* your responsibility too?"

"You're a grown woman, Brit. How do you figure?"

"You're my oldest friend. You got me through my parents' divorce when I was fourteen, my mother's death when I was twenty. You were the first one I told when I lost my virginity. You stood beside me at all three of my weddings and held my hand through the divorces. Don't you ever think that I *can't do this* without you?"

"What are you talking about?"

"I'm not strong like you, Casey. I don't have people around me that care—like you have Cooper and Emma and your sister. Lacey is nothing like Libby. And even your mother, as freaky as she is. I don't have a mother."

"Brit..."

"And J.B.," she continues with a scornful toss of her hair. "Have I ever had a man love me like that? And to think you almost threw it away. The kids. I don't have anyone giving me unconditional love like you do, Casey. I have to work for it. People love me because I make them, and it's hard."

"You don't make me love you," I say awkwardly.

"I don't have anyone else." She enunciates each word. "I had to fight Morgan for you so I just gave up. But I'm your responsibility too because I don't have anyone else. And it hurts—" She pauses and I'm stunned to find her blue eyes have filled with tears. "That you wouldn't want to be here with me. To share this with me."

"It's not that I didn't want to come," I tell her. "It's just hard."

"Sure," she says in a clipped voice. "I get it that I'm not as important to you anymore."

"I was afraid to leave them," I admit in a rush of words. "Not to leave them with J.B., because he couldn't handle it. I thought they'd like being with him, maybe too much. That they'd love him more than me."

Brit narrows her eyes. "You're jealous of your husband? The father of your children? That's even more screwed up than I am."

"Maybe," I laugh. "They're mine. I wanted them more than anyone else, and I need to keep them."

"You're not going to lose your kids because you go away for a couple of nights." Brit laughs but trails off when she catches sight of my expression. "You'll never lose them."

"What if I get shot, like that concert here last year?" I ask, voicing one of my fears.

"I won't let you get shot," Brit says stoutly. "I'm your responsibility, but you're mine too. I won't let anything happen to you.'"

I glance around. "You let me get arrested."

"That was Morgan's fault," Brit says briskly. "I would never have created such a ruckus over a man."

"It was a fun ruckus," Flora admits. I'm so intent on my conversation with Brit that I forgot that she and M.K. are still close behind us and hearing every word. "Hitting that woman felt so good, almost like I've been cleansed." Flora's voice drops, and she glances around with hunched shoulders. "She's not in here, is she?"

"I don't think so," M.K. assures her.

It's then that the officer comes to the bars. "Okay, so no one really wants to press charges, so we're going to have to let you go. Anyone still drunk? Need to sober up?"

Morgan and a hovering Bron are there to greet us with tearful hugs as Brit and I file into the waiting room with the other women.

"I'm so sorry!" she wails, throwing her arms around me.

"Maybe you should apologize to me," Brit huffs. "I'm the one who had her shoes ruined."

"I'm apologizing to you both."

"There's no reason to," I laugh, squeezing Morgan's shoulders. "It's not your fault women get very aggressive when they watch guys dance." I glance up at Bron as I pull away. "Maybe it's yours?"

I'm glad he responds with a grin that tells me he knows I'm joking. There's no way I'm letting Morgan go home with a man without a sense of humour.

"I called J.B.," Morgan says nervously.

"You *what*? Oh god, Morgan." I rest my hand against my forehead. "What did he say?"

"He laughed."

"Really?"

"Said it was his own fault for making you come with us."

Brit smiles at me. "At least we know who is to blame."

CHAPTER SEVENTEEN

> More children should be considered carefully. It's a momentous decision and should not be undertaken lightly.
>
> *A Young Woman's Guide to Raising Obedient Children*
> Dr. Francine Pascal Reid, (1943)

The next afternoon, I sit with Brit on the plane and we talk. About everything. My fears, her fears, what our friendship means to us. I tell her that J.B. wants another baby and she surprises me with her wholehearted support.

"Why wouldn't you want another one? Your kids are amazing and you're a wonderful mother."

"It's a lot to think about."

"You thought too much about it the first time and look what happened. Just see what happens this time," Brit says.

"You sound like a different person," I marvel.

"Things are clearer now," she admits. The flight attendant stops her cart by Brit's seat and asks what we'd like. "I want an iced tea, but a cold one, not some lukewarm can with ice watering it down," Brit orders.

Maybe things are clearer for her, but my Brit can still be a real bitch. But I still love her.

***

J.B. picks me up at the airport. The kids run into my arms, and I sink to the floor, tears in my eyes and heart in my throat as I hold their wriggling bodies.

My babies.

They go to Morgan for hugs, and I'm surprised when Brit opens her arms to them.

I'm even more surprised when Brit accepts J.B.'s offer of a ride home. She crawls into the third row of seats with Morgan, and the kids stare wide-eyed at them.

After I'm home, after the hours spent cuddling the kids and giving them the PG version of the trip, getting them to sleep, and telling J.B. the rest of what happened, I flop on the bed.

"Are you glad you went?" he asks.

I sigh tiredly. "I am. Despite everything. Did I tell you that Bron is coming to visit next week?"

"You told me three times."

"Well, Morgan told me at least that many times." I watch as J.B. strips off his pants. "You know, you could give some of those dancers a run for their money."

He gives his hips a shimmy. "Think so?"

"Know so." I sit up and pull my shirt over my head. "So, are we going to do this?"

"Do what?"

I grin. "Make a baby. Just one this time, so put away whatever super sperm—"

I don't get a chance to finish before J.B. is on the bed with me.

***

Hope you enjoyed more Casey and J.B., and meeting the babies!
Now keep reading for a sneak peek of my new romance
Perfectly Played

I did it! I finally did it! Readers have been asking for a sequel to Un-expecting for years but for some reason, Casey didn't have a story that she wanted me to tell. It's no wonder–with the triplets, she probably had no time for it!

But then it came to me, along with the personalities of Sophie, Lucy, and Ben. I think if I had those kids, I might drink even more than Casey!!

I really hope you enjoy finding out about Casey's Happily Ever After.

In the meantime, here's a sneak peek of something new–the first chapter of my friends-to-lovers romance, *Perfectly Played*. I hope you love Flora and Dean as much as I do!!

Happy Reading!

Holly xo

Keep Reading for

Perfectly Played!

CHAPTER ONE

Perfectly Played
Chapter One

Flora

I hate wearing heels.

Sometimes I think I'm the only woman alive who doesn't appreciate the sleek sexiness of a nice Manolo Blahnik or doesn't melt a bit when I catch sight of the red sole of a Louboutin pump. But a wedding does seem like the place where heels are in order, so I got myself a pair. Nude, patent leather, with a peep toe and four-inch heels. Not stilettos but skinny enough.

Wearing these heels, I take four steps down the aisle of the tiny chapel and stumble. I will later say a loose thread from the well-worn carpet tripped me but at the time I know it's because I can't wear heels.

I do catch myself in time, giving a quick glance to see M.K. clap her hand over her mouth in horror. Ruthie, of course, laughs because she spends her days laughing. But Thomas...

Thomas looks annoyed. Peeved. Irritated.

I take a hesitant step and then another, wishing I had something to hang onto. A father's arm would be best, but Dad is long gone. I'd even settle for one of my brothers to walk me down the aisle, but eloping to Las Vegas, not to mention the giant split between us, kind of puts a damper on that idea.

I could have had a lovely bouquet to hang on to, like the arrangement of creamy-white calla lilies and blue orchids I put together last month, but Thomas insisted he would look after the flowers.

"You work with the things every day," he had said in his soothing voice, the one he uses when he thinks I'm stressing about something. "Let me do this."

Now I'm walking down the aisle with a green leaf that M.K. pulled off a plant in the lobby scrunched in my hand. I'm a *florist* and my fiancé can't remember to buy me flowers.

I take another step and another. I'm within arm's reach, and it would be so nice if Thomas steps forward to meet me halfway. At least reach out a hand.

But he stands there with an expression of annoyance on his face. Why have I never noticed that Thomas loses his looks when he frowns? When the furrow between his eyes deepens, he becomes an old man. Or what he would look like when he was older. Older than me. Quite a bit older than me.

When I make the full stop, the expression of annoyance deepens to pissed off.

"Flora," Thomas hisses, probably thinking I've stopped to say something. I used to be prone to stopping in the middle of the sidewalk or in Loblaws grocery store to loudly announce ideas or plans to everything in my vicinity. I have three brothers and I'm used to making myself heard.

But I haven't done that in years, not since Thomas shushed me on the subway platform when I announced that I *needed* to go see *The Lion King*.

Thomas shushes me a lot.

M.K. and Ruthie stare at me from where they stand at the end of the aisle. Neither one of them hold out their hand to me either, although M.K. gives me an expectant nod. But I can't move. I stand there not three feet from the place I'm supposed to be in to say "I do" to the love of my life.

Is he?

He didn't buy me flowers.

He knows I wanted flowers at my wedding. I love flowers.

He's *never* bought me flowers.

Suddenly the words are in my mouth like that little bit of bring-up I get when Thomas makes me drink a smoothie. "I can't marry you."

The words are drowned out by the "Wedding March" so I say it louder. "I can't marry you." This time the couple in the lobby can hear me.

"Flora, stop it." There is no doubt that Thomas is frustrated. Annoyed, irritated, aggravated—there's no sense going through the thesaurus because all the words are the same.

He is *pissed*.

And suddenly I don't care.

"No."

"Flora." The way he says my name is a warning, a clear indication he's angry. I've spent the past eight years doing all I can to avoid his anger.

I'm done now.

"I can't do this," I say. "I don't want to marry you, Thomas. I thought I did, but I don't. Not now. Not...ever."

Thomas shakes his head, looking a bit like a wet dog forced to come in from the rain. "*You* wanted this. I was perfectly happy with how things were, but *you* wanted more. You *always* want more."

"I *deserve* more." I hold out my leaf, which left a green smear on my hand. "I deserve flowers."

"This is because I didn't get you flowers?"

"Oh, god, don't start with the flowers with her," Ruthie says under her breath.

Thankfully, Thomas ignores her. "Stop being a child, Flora."

"I'm twenty-nine and have my own business. You're the only one who thinks I'm a child."

Someone finally moves and it's the justice of the peace, still holding his prayer book with both hands. "If the blessed event isn't going to take place, I do have others that need the space." He looks down his nose at me like this is a prank gone wrong.

"I can't marry him," I repeat. "I'm sorry, but I can't. I thought I could; I thought it was what I wanted but now that I'm here and you're standing there looking so annoyed with me and I don't have any flowers that I—"

"Yes, we know, Flora," M.K. says, stepping forward to take my hand. M.K. is always patient and calm except for when she isn't. "You're not going to marry him. We need to get out of here, then."

"I don't believe you!" Thomas erupts. "That's it?"

The words I should say dry up in my mouth. "I can't. I don't know what else to say."

"You've ruined everything."

"No, I think that was *you*," Ruthie says, reaching for my other hand.

With a final look of disgust, Thomas storms past us like I'm nothing more than a slow-moving pedestrian in his rush to get to work.

UNEXPECTINGLY HAPPILY EVER AFTER

"Jackass," Ruthie says loudly. "Don't let the door hit you in the ass on the way out."

The three of us turn and watch Thomas disappear into the lobby. Then he's gone.

"That's it?" Ruthie asks.

"He's gone," M.K. marvels. I'm not imagining the relief in her voice.

"Ladies." A glance over my shoulder shows the justice of the peace with a thunderous expression that no man of God should ever wear.

"Has he been paid yet?" Ruthie mutters.

M.K. squeezes my hand. "Let's get out of here."

Suddenly I have the urge to run, run away from the chapel and the justice of the peace and what is undoubtedly going to be on the top ten list of all-time worst days. Hiking up the dress I bought off the rack at Nordstrom for forty percent off, I run down the aisle to the lobby, with M.K. and Ruthie hot on my heels.

And then the toe of my shoe really does catch on a loose thread on the carpet, sending me careening right into a man standing in the doorway of the chapel.

"Jesus!" My face smashes into a broad back and I grab on to him to keep from falling.

"What the—?" He looks over his shoulder, yet another man annoyed with me. I get a glimpse of bright blue eyes and a well-trimmed beard the colour of fall leaves before I push away.

"Flora, come on! How could you not see him?" Ruthie is laughing as she rushes up, blonde braids dancing like crazed snakes. "He's like the size of a tree."

The man turns, towering over me by almost a foot. Tree indeed.

"Are you all right?"

He looks nice, I think irrationally. Cute, especially with the beard.

Like it has a mind of its own, my hand reaches up and touches his cheek. My fingers trace his jawline, the wiry, reddish hair softer than it looks.

His eyes widen. "What—?"

I gasp and drop my hand. "Get out of my way" I demand. "I have to get out of here."

He steps aside and I run down the street, with Ruthie and M.K. chasing after me.

Grab your copy and find out what happens with Flora and Dean in Perfectly Played

Made in United States
North Haven, CT
03 August 2024